UNCOMMON SACRIFICE

WAR GIRL SERIES

MARION KUMMEROW

CONTENTS

CHAPTER 1: STAN

Somewhere in Poland, November 1944

Stanislaw Zdanek, called Stan, and his friend Bartosz stepped into the partially destroyed building keeping their weapons at the ready.

Adrenaline surged through Stan's body, sending his heart throbbing against his chest. It felt good to actually fight and not merely sabotage the Germans who'd ruled Poland with an iron fist for six years. After years of hiding, the members of the Polish Home Army had finally joined the open battle against the Nazis.

"Clear!" Stan shouted and waved at his comrades.

They stepped out from their cover and searched the rest of the ruins for German soldiers. But they had left earlier in the day, taking to their heels with the overpowering Red Army approaching further south.

Slowly, civilians crawled out from their damaged houses, faces smeared with dirt, but wearing happy smiles.

Even after witnessing the liberations of dozens of Polish villages, a lump formed in Stan's throat. *That's it. We're free again. The Nazi vermin is done for.*

Obviously he'd never show weakness in the presence of his comrades and so he swallowed down the emotions that threatened to overwhelm him. After the devastating defeat of the Warsaw Uprising, it had taken the Home Army quite some time to regroup and boost morale.

But now they were back to free their country and avenge the deaths of hundreds of thousands in the former capital – Warsaw had been razed to the ground. If Stan could believe the stories told, there wasn't a single building standing in the city that had previously hosted close to a million citizens.

A peachy young woman, undernourished like most everyone in war-torn Europe, approached the group of soldiers and pressed a kiss on Stan's whiskered cheek.

"Thank you for liberating us," she said and cast him a smile.

His comrades cheered and demanded kisses as well, until their commanding officer stopped the spectacle. They left a few posts on the watch in the village and retreated for some much-needed food and sleep in the empty concrete school building.

"You'd better get that beard trimmed or you'll never score another kiss," a comrade teased.

"Yeah, did you see her look of disgust?" another one chimed in.

Stan glanced around and scrubbed a hand over his stubbled jaw. He wasn't the only one with a dirt-smeared face and a badly trimmed beard. But freedom seemed to top cleanliness in priorities right now, and the Home Army fighters clearly had hero-appeal for the local women.

Cracking his neck a few times and running the same hand over his cropped blond hair, he tossed the offender a smirk. "You're just jealous of my good looks."

Everyone laughed and continued to wolf down the food generously provided by the villagers. Stan wiped his mouth, groaned and dropped flat on the bare floor. Months ago, he'd stopped bothering to take off his boots and he was sound asleep before his head even hit the pillow provided by his backpack.

Shouts of alarm jerked him from sleep and Stan grabbed the rifle propped up at his side before shooting to his feet, eyes still closed.

"Red Army approaching!" someone shouted and a sigh of relief went through the room. The Red Army was on their side; they had nothing to fear from the Russians. After a few short greetings, the Russian commanding officer approached Stan's superior. Stan couldn't understand their whispered words, but the expression on his superior's face didn't augur well.

"What do you think they want?" Stan asked Bartosz, who stood by his side.

"Probably some quarrel about who gets to claim the praise," Bartosz said, rather disinterested.

"Everyone listen," the Russian officer spoke up and waited until all the noise had died down in the room. "We're offering everyone here the opportunity to voluntarily join the great Soviet Army."

A whispering went through the ranks amongst those who understood Russian.

"I'll be damned if I join their army," Stan murmured to Bartosz while a Russian soldier translated the officer's words to the group.

The new soldier added, "Those who don't take up our generous offer will have to lay down their weapons; they are hereby arrested."

Before his men could protest, Stan's superior said, "As I see it, there's not much of a choice involved. Do what is best for Poland. You won't be of any use to our country in a Siberian Gulag."

"So who's with us against the Nazis?" the Russian officer asked.

Stan barely reined in his temper and groaned beneath his breath. "Obviously, we're against the Nazis but that doesn't make me a friend of these bastards."

"Same here," Bartosz whispered.

Looking into the faces of his comrades, Stan noticed that none of them liked the *generous* offer the Russians had extended. But in spite of their disdain, one by one his fellow soldiers moved forward to sign their names on the list for joining the Red Army.

More than one of the men had to swallow down a lump before they provided their names and handed over the red and white armband identifying them as Home Army.

Stan clenched his fists, and then his jaw, ready to pounce at the Russian officer and take down at least two or three of the hateful bastards before going down himself. Bartosz though, had known his friend long enough to be aware of Stan's short fuse and put a hand on his arm, whispering, "Don't."

"Some choice," Stan growled between clenched teeth.

"Right, man. But I for one want to live and fight. You with me?"

"I'm doing this only because they force my hand, but you can be sure I'll slit their throats at my first opportunity." The next moment Stan felt Bartosz's hand in his back, pushing him forward.

"We want to volunteer," Bartosz announced and put both of their names on the list.

Stan glared at his friend but reluctantly admitted that joining the Red Army was a far cry better than ending up in Siberia. Technically, they were allies, so it wasn't like defecting to the enemy. He'd fight under the Soviet banner alright, but at the first opportunity, he'd turn on his heels and escape.

CHAPTER 2: PETER

Fallingbostel, Germany

P eter Wolf, also known as Piotr Zdanek, sat behind a rickety table covered in lists.

"Name?" he asked in Russian.

The man's shoulders slumped. "Dmitri Bylikov."

"Nationality?"

"Russian."

Peter checked the appropriate box. "Rank?"

"Private."

Peter nodded, jotting down the rest of the information on the list and putting a number beside it. *"Russenlager.* Go to the next table and they'll assign you a blanket and mess kit." He handed the newcomer a piece of cloth with the letters "KG", which stood for *Kriegsgefangener,* prisoner of war. "And put this on the back of your tunic."

The Russian prisoner barely raised his head as he took the sign and trotted off to the next table.

Peter had been at the camp in Fallingbostel several weeks already. Taken captive after the surrender of the Polish Home Army in the Warsaw Uprising, he'd been tasked by the Germans with registering the newcomers. Apparently, they considered speaking fluent Polish, German, English and Russian an asset.

As an officer of the Polish Home Army, Peter was exempt from work according to the Geneva Convention, but the Nazis didn't care much about international treaties. And he actually preferred sitting at his table all day long registering newcomers to sitting in front of the barracks with nothing else to do than stare at the sky or sleep.

The new job came with perks, like extra food, for which he was incredibly thankful. Even with slightly bigger rations than the rest, hunger gnawed at his intestines day and night. He didn't even want to imagine what the other prisoners, and especially the poor Russian and Italian souls, had to endure.

As far as prisoner camps went, Fallingbostel, or Stalag XI B (357), was certainly not jolly, but he'd seen worse during his time working as a driver for Professor Scherer in Berlin, a scientist who socialized with all the top Nazis. Most of the close to one hundred thousand captured soldiers from about a dozen nationalities toiled in one of the Arbeitskommandos, the labor squads. While the work was certainly backbreaking, at least those who worked got to eat.

As in any camp, prisoners in Fallingbostel were separated by nationality, and those with a superior nationality according to Hitler's racial ideology – Westerners with

Aryan heritage – had much better prospects of surviving their ordeal than those of inferior or Slavic nationalities.

At least the Germans had stuck to their word and treated the Home Army prisoners from the Warsaw Uprising as POWs and not as partisans.

"Step forward," he called out to the next man in line. The man attempted to stand up straight and adopt a pain-free expression, but failed miserably and limped the few steps to Peter's table.

"Name?"

"Vasily Bulychev."

Peter switched to Russian. "Nationality?"

"Russian." The prisoner showed no surprise that Peter spoke Russian.

"Rank?"

"Private."

Out of habit, Peter wrote *Russenlager* beside the man's name and the prisoner number on the list. Lately most every newcomer had been Russian, save for the odd Englishman in between. But then he looked up and asked, "What's wrong with your leg?"

"Gunshot in the thigh."

Peter motioned one of the medics forward. "This prisoner," he said, glancing at the list, "Vasily Bulychev, has a gunshot wound."

The medic, a prisoner himself, nodded and squatted down. He pushed apart the tattered remains of the uniform and sucked in a breath. "He'll need to go to the camp hospital."

"Take him there," Peter said and crossed out *Russenlager* on the list to put Camp Hospital instead, and took a deep breath before he looked up at the next prisoner and started the process all over again.

Peter didn't like the role he played, but under the current circumstances this task helped to ensure the survival of his comrades. The camp commandant had discovered that Peter's influence on the other prisoners made life so much easier for everyone involved, and would often grant requests for better treatment in exchange for good behavior.

Still, each morning Peter woke hoping that today would be the day of his liberation. Then he would see his German wife, Anna, again and if God was benevolent, he might even be reunited with what remained of his Polish family. His son Janusz, his brother Stan, and his sister Katrina.

With the war winding down and the Allies assured of winning, the Nazis still stubbornly held on for dear life, even mobilizing the last reserves, boys aged fourteen to sixteen and ancient men above forty years old, in a crazy effort they called Volkssturm, storm of the people.

Peter scoffed. Most ordinary German people had long given up on the idea that Germany could win this awful war instigated by a delusional man – a master manipulator whom they'd unwittingly believed for the longest time.

CHAPTER 3: ANNA

Berlin

Inhaling a ragged breath, Anna Klausen crawled from the bomb shelter as she turned to survey the damage the last air raid had brought upon this part of the city. At the age of twenty-two, Anna had known nothing but war since becoming an adult.

Please God, end this horrible war before it's too late.

Even worse, her husband Peter had been taken prisoner of war after traveling to Warsaw to fight for his country in what would be known as the Warsaw Uprising. A disastrous undertaking that killed hundreds of thousands – civilians and combatants alike.

She pushed her straight blond hair behind her ears and surveyed her surroundings. Several of the employee housing blocks next to the Charité clinic where she worked as a nurse lay in ruins. The stones lay crumbled and scattered across the grounds, smoke continuing to rise from within. Anna shook her head and fought down the tears forming in her blue eyes as she slowly approached the location of the building that had been her home only hours before.

"It's nothing but trash," Janusz murmured by her side.

"You're right."

She ruffled the boy's dark and dusted hair, giving him a crooked smile. She'd been thrust into motherhood less than a month ago when her sister Lotte had arrived in Berlin with Peter's presumed-dead son. Being the stepmother and sole provider for a twelve-year-old boy, whom she'd never met before, definitely presented its challenges, even with such a well-behaved child.

He grinned back at her with his glacial blue eyes, sending a stab through her stomach. Those eyes reminded her of her husband, Peter, every time she looked at them. Apart from Peter's eyes, Jan had inherited the dark hair and high cheekbones from his Jewish mother Ludmila, Peter's first wife.

Another stab in the heart reminded Anna that Ludmila had died at the hands of the Nazis in the Lodz Ghetto. Jan had miraculously survived thanks to the intervention of Ludmila's brave sister, Agnieska, and some mysterious German soldier named Richard.

Richard...

Anna hadn't heard from her brother with the same name as the man who'd saved Jan in several months, which meant her mind often drifted to horrible possibilities. Richard could be injured, or worse. A tortured sigh escaped her chest and Janusz turned his head, pushing his small hand into hers.

11

Anna pulled her mind from the depressing thoughts and back to the equally depressing task that lay ahead of them. "Let's see if we can salvage some of our things and then we'll go to my mother's place."

Janusz nodded, his eyes reflecting a maturity far beyond his years. "I wish this war would end..."

Anna shook her head and placed her finger on her lips. Her sister Lotte's boyfriend Johann, a Leutnant in the Wehrmacht, had provided Janusz with false gentile papers, turning him into the Aryan boy Jan Wagner. But she lived in constant fear he might be found out.

As a half-Jewish Pole, his chances of survival were devastating should this happen. And hers too, for the crime of harboring an *enemy of the Reich*. She scoffed. How could a well-behaved, friendly boy like Jan be an enemy of the Reich?

The boy nodded his approval to her unspoken request and squared his shoulders as they walked toward the smoldering remains of their home. Having lived hidden in the Lodz Ghetto for months he knew all about ducking his head and keeping his mouth shut. Anna sighed again. What kind of upbringing was this for a child?

More and more people crawled out of the common bomb shelter on the Charité grounds and hurried towards the remains of their buildings, ignoring the smoke rising from the ashes and the burning debris scattered across the grounds. Thankfully, the hospital part had survived, and Anna knew they'd have an influx of new patients after the latest raid. But first she had to get Jan to safety with her mother.

When they arrived at the place where their apartment

had once been she spied several articles of clothing that, while covered in dust and debris, looked to be intact and just in need of a good washing. She carefully tucked them into a bag she'd liberated from the rubble several minutes earlier, telling Jan to do the same with the items he found.

An hour later, a few meager possessions tucked away in the bag, Anna and Jan began the long walk to where her mother and her sister Ursula lived with baby Eveline.

They arrived at the apartment and knocked on the door, since the electric bell had long since stopped working. Electricity had become an unreliable utility, coming and going, but mostly going. Another of the hardships of war. Anna cursed once again the delusional man responsible for all of this turmoil. If only the people of Germany had known... although she didn't hold much hope that most people would have stood up to fight against such injustice. They resembled sheeple, running behind their charismatic shepherd, afraid of the growling herding dogs if they dared to stray from the center of the flock.

"Anna, Jan. What a surprise!" Ursula greeted them when she opened the door, but after a second look at the disheveled state of them, the smile vanished from her face, "What happened?"

"The usual. The awful Englishman dropping his gifts."

"Come in." Ursula pursed her lips, conflicted. Since she'd fallen in love with one of the hated English bomber pilots, the topic irritated her.

"Our apartment complex is a complete loss and we need to find another place to live," Anna said.

Ursula looked at the bag Anna carried and said, "It looks like this place is getting crowded again. Is this all you have?"

"This and the things we already have deposited here." Most Berliners had suitcases with essentials deposited with friends or relatives in different areas of the city for occasions like this one. Anna had never thought she'd have to depend on one of her emergency suitcases. She suppressed a heavy sigh as she thought of all the things lost to the shelling. Not that she owned things of material value, but suddenly the emotional attachment weighed heavily on her soul.

Ursula glanced at her sister and without hearing the words, she seemed to understand Anna's desolate state of mind. "Despite everything, Mutter will be glad to have you and Jan here so she can fuss over you."

Anna groaned. That had been one of the reasons she'd left the family apartment to live in the employment housing. That, and the dangerous journey to and from work.

"Jan, why don't you put your things down in the nursery and then clean yourself up? You look like Max and Moritz after falling into the flour box." Ursula giggled at Jan's indignant face while trying to dust himself off. Anna joined the laughter, wondering how she could still be laughing like a silly girl after what had just happened.

After pouring herself a glass of water, she dropped on a kitchen chair. Silly giggles helped her cope with this awfulness. It didn't help to lament. And she couldn't very well live day in, day out with her lips pressed into a thin line. That would mean giving up and letting the darkness win. No, as long as there was even a sliver of hope, she'd giggle like the silliest adolescent.

Ursula joined her at the kitchen table, while Jan dashed off to the bathroom to take a shower. "Be glad you and Jan are still alive. You did rescue his papers, didn't you?"

"Off course. Do you think me stupid?" Anna snapped, regretting her reaction in the same moment. "Sorry. It was a tough day. He has his papers on him day and night. Without them he'd be dead within days."

Anna sipped at her water and leaned back, looking at her sister. "I must find a way of writing him," she murmured.

Ursula reached across the table and grabbed Anna's hand. "You know that is not possible. Peter is a prisoner of war. It's forbidden to engage with them. If they find out..." Anna knew all this. Her husband was a prisoner, an enemy, a Pole, a subhuman. Trying to contact him would sentence both of them to death.

"There has to be some way," she insisted.

"I wish there was, but it's too dangerous. Right now, you need to focus on Jan. You're the only family he has left."

"I'm not even real family. And he has you, and Mutter," Anna said. Her mother had never really approved of Peter, a man living under a false identity, as a son-in-law, but she'd instantly taken to her new grandson. Jan and his grandmother adored each other.

"And we will take care of him, should...you know...but it's best to be cautious." A squeaking sound interrupted them and Ursula got up from the table. "I need to go check on the baby."

Anna nodded, not paying much attention to her sister's departure. She heard Jan leave the bathroom and scuffle

15

around the small apartment, unpacking the few belongings they'd salvaged from the rubble of their previous home. She should be doing the same, but right now she couldn't focus on anything except the need to contact Peter and let him know she and Jan were safe.

When Ursula returned with baby Eveline cradled in her arms, Anna said, "I'm going to join the Red Cross."

"You...what?" Understanding hit Ursula and she said, "That would never work."

"Of course it would. They let members of the Red Cross inside the prison camps to check up on the prisoners."

Ursula handed the baby to Anna and heated milk on the stove. "The *International* Red Cross. And there's no guarantee that you'd be visiting his prison camp. Besides, what would be your excuse for quitting your job as a nurse to join the Red Cross?"

"I wouldn't need one." Anna kissed baby Evie's small forehead and held the five-month-old against her shoulder.

"Yes, you would," Ursula insisted. "The minute you requested to visit a specific prisoner's camp, they'd suspect something."

Anna sighed, digesting the truth of her sister's words. "I'll find a way. I just don't know how yet, but there's always a way."

Ursula filled the bottle, tested the temperature on her wrist and handed it to Anna. "I don't agree, but knowing your stubbornness, if there is a way, you'll be the one to find it."

Anna adjusted the baby in her arms and stuck the bottle in her mouth. "Aunt Anna will find it, don't you worry your pretty little head about it, Evie. I can't wait for you to meet

Uncle Peter. He's going to fall in love with you just like everyone else has."

She closed her eyes for a moment, firming her resolve to do whatever it took to contact Peter. It was the least she could do. Not only was he her husband, but also her best friend aside from her family. And while she was at it, she'd find a way of getting him out. Then he just had to resume his fake German identity as Peter Wolf, driver of Professor Scherer.

CHAPTER 4: STAN

S tan and Bartosz snuck around the eastern edge of the town, accompanied by a dozen of their new Soviet *comrades*, intending to overrun the assumed enemy command center while the rest of the unit swarmed out to engage the pockets of Germans in the vicinity.

But when they entered the stone building, it was completely empty. Their group leader stopped cold in his tracks. Stan's senses shot into high alert, instantly focusing his vision and amplifying his hearing. Then he heard it: Footfalls. Hissed commands. Gunfire.

Stan groaned. They'd been set up and walked into the trap like mice looking for cheese. Trapped inside the building that was taking serious mortar fire from a German tank ambling down the street.

"We need to get out of here before this building comes down around our ears," Stan hissed.

"We're surrounded, *minetschik*. There's no way out," one of the Russians said.

Stan spoke enough Russian to understand the swear word and glared at the other man. Since the fateful moment he'd been forced to join the Red Army, he'd been waiting for an opportunity to desert. But that would have to wait. Right now, he was solely concerned with survival.

The group leader seemed to share Stan's opinion and said, "Everyone form up at the back entrance. On my signal, rush out in pairs. Go round the village and join up with the rest of the battalion in the south."

As a plan, Stan wasn't convinced that it would work, but anything was better than sitting inside waiting to be plucked off like ducks on a glassy pond. Stan translated to Bartosz, who still lacked Russian language skills.

"You think that'll work?" Bartosz murmured, but they both knew it was their only chance. Sometimes the odds weren't stacked high enough in favor of a strategy.

"We'll get through this together," Stan said, as much to bolster up himself as his friend.

They gathered at the back door and at their group leader's signal they dashed to the right of the building. Stan crouched behind a low wall, aiming his machine gun at the Nazi soldiers swarming the rubble left by the fierce fighting earlier today. Only the devil knew where they'd suddenly appeared from.

He squeezed the trigger and watched one of the Nazis fall to the side. *Nice shot*, he thought. A fleeting blast of pleasure hit his chest right before his neck hair rose and tingled. His throbbing pulse and roiling gut told him to turn his head. Slowly, he pivoted only to stare into the muzzle of a German Schmeisser. *Shit!*

"*Waffe weg und Hände hoch!*" Drop your weapon and put

your hands up, the German soldier demanded. Stan did what was requested. The soldier holding him at gunpoint was a boy, not more than eighteen years of age, fear clearly written across his face.

Someone pulled a trigger and Stan flinched. But much to his surprise it was the young German who fell like a tree with a loud flop.

"Go!" someone shouted and Stan ran for his life. He managed to reach the other side of the street with bullets whizzing past his ears. Somehow, he jumped across a hedge and ducked headfirst into a ditch. Bartosz followed, just as another round of mortar fire pulverized the hedge. With a pounding heart, Stan lay crumpled in the ditch listening to the sounds of battle explode around them. Judging from the prevalent language in the screams and shouts, he guessed the Germans were finishing off the Russians. After a while the noise died down, but he and Bartosz remained immobile. If they pretended to be dead, they might stay undetected.

After an endless amount of time, Stan peeked out from his cover onto the deserted street. "Seems like everyone's gone," he said to Bartosz, who raised his helmeted head to check for himself.

"And now? Go back and find our unit, or...?"

Stan knew that Bartosz hated being part of the Red Army as much as he did, and the prospect to defect and find a Home Army unit tempted them both. They were now approximately three quarters of a mile from the point where they'd first entered the town and were supposed to meet up again with their unit.

"I heard there's Home Army about ten miles up north. Think we could make a dash for them?" Bartosz asked.

Anything was better than being ridiculed and harassed by their so-called comrades. Animosities between Soviets and Poles had been rampant for centuries and weren't easily overcome. Witnessing how those depraved bastards treated the Polish civilians, and especially the women, had only deepened Stan's hate for everything Soviet.

They nodded at each other and then crawled from the ditch, walking crouched down until they reached the next building. Stan kept his eyes trained from 9 o'clock to 3 o'clock ahead, while Bartosz covered the same area behind. It reminded him of the good old days, living in the forest and sabotaging the Nazis. Stan and Bartosz had been friends for close to a decade and they'd been fighting in several partisan units together since Hitler's invasion five years ago.

Only empty fields lay ahead of them once they reached the end of the village. As they hadn't seen another soul since leaving their ditch, Stan pointed at a tree in the distance. Bartosz nodded. After so many years together, they didn't need words to communicate.

About halfway to the tree, a white-hot streak of fire shot down Stan's leg, making him cry out in pain. Bartosz stopped and looked back, but Stan waved him forward. Adrenaline pumping through his veins, he ignored the pain and kept running, panic urging him forward. Minutes later, he arrived at the tree and crumpled against the trunk. His hand reached for his left leg and felt hot liquid. Blood pumped from the gunshot wound and soaked his uniform with a dark red spot that became bigger with each heartbeat. He pressed his hand onto the wound, the thrumming pulse in his ear drowning out all other sounds.

Bartosz rummaged in his backpack and found a dressing that he used to apply a pressure bandage to Stan's leg.

Stan leaned against the tree, the pain crashing in waves across his body with every beat of his heart. He gritted his teeth so hard he feared they'd fall out. Oblivious to his surroundings, he fought the black stars dancing in front of his eyes and sighed with relief when Bartosz stopped mistreating his leg.

"Get up," Bartosz said.

Stan tried, but didn't manage more than a few inches before he fell back on his bottom. "I can't. You go and find the Home Army unit."

"I'm not leaving you, stubborn asshole. Here, take my hand. I'm gonna carry you."

Stan had lost plenty of weight over the years, but he was still a big man; Bartosz wouldn't have a whiff of a chance to escape with the additional load on his back. Looking into Bartosz's face, Stan gave a half-grin at his friend's determination. He would have done the same. Only a bastard would leave his wounded friend behind.

They'd walked less than five minutes when German shouts rang through the air. Since neither of them was in a position to fight, Bartosz turned around, raising his hands, while Stan slid down his back and somehow managed to hold himself upright on his good leg.

A group of Wehrmacht soldiers approached them and kicked their weapons away with mud-coated boots. One of them, standing a short distance away, motioned to Bartosz and forced him to kneel with his hands locked behind his head.

Deprived of the firm support Bartosz had presented, Stan swayed on his one leg, unable to put weight on the wounded one. He tried desperately to keep his equilibrium but when forced to raise his hands, he fell facedown into the field. Big hands grabbed his shoulders and rolled him over. Stan let out a loud cry of distress and thought he'd faint with the unbearable pain.

"*Der sieht schlimm aus,*" the German said, a trace of pity in his voice. This one looks bad.

Having grown up near Lodz where many Germans lived, Stan spoke fluent German and Russian, in addition to his native language Polish and some English he'd learned at school.

They discussed whether to leave him to die. Stan held his breath. In the end, someone put in a good word for him and they decided that the other prisoner should carry the wounded fellow to the camp. Stan must have passed out on the way, because he woke up cooped up in the back of a lorry.

Disoriented, reality caught up to him with the next bump in the road and the painful reminder of the wound in his leg. He glanced down and watched blood oozing through the bandage. He groaned with the excruciating pain and his vision became dizzy again. Another captured Russian soldier with a red cross on his sleeve bent over him and removed the bandage, just to secure it again with more pressure.

The soldier murmured something in Russian, but Stan didn't care to listen. Without medical treatment, he'd bleed out. Another wave of intolerable pain washed over him and he prayed to lose consciousness. No such luck. Every bump in the road rattled through his body, electric zings of agony reaching every last cell.

Bartosz appeared by his side saying, "You still alive, man?"

"Barely."

"Hold on. You're not gonna die on me here."

A short time later, the lorry stopped, and voices yelled German commands to hurry down the lorry. Stan and two other wounded prisoners were unloaded and brought to a field hospital while the rest had to camp outside in something that looked like a cage.

"He won't make it through the night," one medic said.

"Or he'll die on the train. That's not our concern. We're just doing our job. We treat all the captured soldiers as best as we can."

Stan decided to make it through the night, just to prove them wrong.

The next morning, his eyes snapped open to the rising sun. The bleeding in his thigh seemed to have stopped and while he still couldn't get up, he was alive.

Together with the other prisoners he was crowded onto a train. As infection infiltrated his gunshot wound, fever took up residence in his body. He passed the three-day journey mostly in delirium with beads of sweat peppering his forehead. When the unloading jostled him back to awareness, it barely registered in his brain. Someone dumped him onto the bare ground in a tent already filled with groaning and whimpering men.

Stan didn't care. Between the excruciating pain and the ghastly thirst his brain had stopped working. Nobody bothered to offer him water or even help him with his bodily needs. Since the debilitating injury and the high fever left him unable to do anything but lie there and shake, he came to a point where he simply let it flow.

Delirious with fever, he slipped in and out of consciousness. Throughout the ordeal, only one thought penetrated the fog in his brain. He hoped to see his brother Peter again – in this world or the next one.

CHAPTER 5: PETER

Peter slumped on the earth in front of his barracks as he observed a dreadful-looking bunch of ragged men unloaded from the nearby train ramp. Actually, those were the lucky ones. They didn't have to walk the five miles from the main train station in the town of Fallingbostel.

Hunger gnawing at his stomach, he somehow gathered the energy to stand up and trudge toward his table in the reception area, where the supervising German soldiers had already taken up residence. Most of them were more accommodating, but today one of the vicious guards, Müller, was on duty. Peter swallowed a groan as his stomach tightened.

The older guard, a so-called *Landesschütze,* had received a debilitating injury during the Russian campaign in 1942, which confined him to serving his country as a prison camp guard. Müller hated the Russians with a passion and treated them accordingly.

Peter slipped into his seat ignoring the glare Müller sent

him, but instinctively ducking his head between his shoulders. The brute liked to make extensive use of his stick and it didn't take much to attract his wrath.

More Russians. Poor lads, Peter thought as he started to ask them for name, nationality and unit. Conditions were bad everywhere in the camp, but in the separated area a few hundred yards away where the Russians were held, conditions were inhuman, and Peter often wondered how most of them managed to survive day to day.

Another dirty and disheveled man stepped in front of Peter. He was tall and his face, while still showing evidence of his youth, looked weary. His big, bleak eyes lacked expression.

"Name?" Peter asked in Russian.

"Bartosz Jaworski."

"Nationality?"

"Polish."

"What?" Peter all but dropped his pen as he looked at the man in Russian uniform claiming to be a Pole. "Why are you with the Red Army?" he asked, switching to Polish.

"Because those bas—" Bartosz said, but stopped and winced when Müller's stick hit him on the head.

"What's that bloody *Rotarmist* saying?" Müller demanded to know.

"He's in fact a Pole and should be—" The stick flew down on Peter's shoulders.

"Bloody bastards all of them. Makes no difference to me. Put him in with the rest of the Russians."

"But—" Another punch knocked the breath out of Peter's chest and he quickly wrote *Russenlager* besides Bartosz' name, but made a mental note to try and relocate him later to the Polish barracks.

After processing all the newcomers except for those who couldn't walk on their own, Peter wanted to drop to the ground and sleep for the rest of his life – that or eat until the incessant gnawing ache in his stomach went away. Unfortunately, neither choice was possible. Instead he walked over to the place where the Russians were gathered waiting to be taken to their area of the camp.

Since he was about half a head taller than most of the others, Peter easily spotted Bartosz and approached him. "Hey! Bartosz! Come here!"

"What d'you want?" Bartosz looked up, confused, but his eyes lit up when he recognized the man who'd processed him earlier.

"Why are you with the Red Army?" Peter came straight to the point.

Bartosz shrugged and lowered his voice. "Making a pact with one devil to fight another one."

"So you chose to fight with them to liberate Poland?" Peter couldn't fathom how any patriot in his right mind would join the Red Army, but in this war sacrifices had to be made.

"It wasn't by choice." Bartosz spat on the ground. "The bastards forced us to join their ranks, or be shipped off to Siberia. And now I'll die amidst enemies."

"First you'll suffer like an animal." Peter's blood boiled with rage for his countryman and his mind seethed with a few choice words for both the Nazis and the Russians who trampled back and forth across Poland as if it were their sandbox. "Are there more Poles in your transport?"

Bartosz's eyes clouded over. "All were killed in my unit, except for my friend and me. But there could be others."

"Where's your friend?" Peter asked, wondering why he hadn't come across the other Polish soldier during the registration.

"Dunno. He was shot a week ago and was more dead than alive when we arrived here."

"Hmm. They probably took him to the field hospital." Peter bit his lip, deciding not to tell Bartosz what they really did with the cases they deemed incurable. "Keep your pecker up and don't get into trouble. I'll see if I can get you relocated to the Polish barracks. Not that ours are particularly cozy either, but at least you are considered a human."

Peter turned on his heel and walked to his barracks, where he flopped onto the ground, heaving like a locomotive. Without proper food for weeks, even a one-hundred-yard walk seemed like running a marathon.

A comrade had saved him a cup of coffee and a piece of bread from dinner earlier. The coffee was some stinking, putrid, brown liquid that tasted more like dishwater than anything else and the bread was a stone-hard, dark piece of something that only became edible when dunked into said *coffee*. He chewed the bread and imagined eating a full meal of roast pork with mashed potatoes and cabbage. The images helped to gulp down the disgusting food.

After dinner he fought for the energy to get up again and walk over to the commandant's office to try and put in a good word for the Polish prisoners. The conditions in the Russian part of the camp weren't fit for an animal, let alone a human. If Bartosz's friend was injured as badly as Peter guessed, he'd be lucky if he had survived the day in the dirty barracks used to house the Russian injured.

He knocked on the commandant's door and then entered at the man's request.

"Zdanek? Any problems out there?"

"No, sir," Peter said, pondering how to best broach the subject. The commandant wasn't particularly cruel or sadistic, but he still was a Nazi and valued Hitler's ideas. "Another transport of Red Army soldiers arrived this morning."

"I know. And I'm aware their quarters are overcrowded already."

"That is not why I'm here, sir. But some of them aren't Russians."

"Russians, Ukrainians, Cossacks, they're all the same. Soviets – that's what they call themselves nowadays, as if it would make a difference," the commandant scoffed.

Peter weighed his words carefully. "I agree. The Soviets are as much a threat to Poland as they are to Germany, but there are some Poles among this transport."

"Poles?" The commandant wrinkled his nose. As members of the Slavic race, Polish people were considered inferior to the Aryan race, but still above the Jews and the Soviets.

"Yes, I personally verified this claim and…" A little white lie would help make his case. "They fought in the Warsaw Uprising before being forced into the ranks of the Soviet Army. And as such they should be treated according to the Geneva Convention, as was promised by Erich von dem Bach in the capitulation treaty."

The commandant kept quiet for a minute, apparently

thinking over the request. Then he shrugged and said, "I don't care either way. If you wish, have the confirmed Poles transferred to the Polish area.

"Thank you, sir. May I have permission to look over the processing logs from today?"

The commandant waved over to the stack of lists in the corner and seated himself at his desk to attend to whatever work he had to do. Minutes later the secretary brought a glass of water and an apple for the commandant. Peter's mouth watered and his stomach squeezed painfully with every crunching bite the commandant took from the apple. Peter had almost forgotten how an apple tasted, since the food in the camp consisted basically of stone-hard bread, potatoes and turnips.

Peter did his best to focus on the names on the list, despite the distracting sounds of munching that made him only more aware of his debilitating hunger. He noticed several Polish names, including a Stanislaw Zdanek. His brother's name. His heart missed a beat or two as he read the name, but he tried not to jump to conclusions and reminded himself that both Zdanek and Stanislaw were very common Polish names. He jotted down the prisoner numbers and presented them to the commandant, asking for permission to verify their nationality and transfer them to the Polish area.

The commandant took the telephone receiver and dialed a number to ask the guard on duty to bring the prisoners to the interrogation room. Then, he took up his apple core and struck out his arm to toss it into the dustbin when he noticed Peter's hungry stare glued to his every movement.

"You want this?" the commandant asked in disbelief and

at Peter's nod he tossed him the apple core. Peter shoved it into his pocket, unwilling to humiliate himself further and devour the discarded food in front of the other man's eyes.

When Peter arrived back in his barracks he observed a pack of prisoners arriving from the Russian part of the camp. He counted seven, but there should be eight.

All of the young men looked like ancients, hollow looks in their eyes testifying they had seen things they would never be able to forget. The young man called Bartosz came up to Peter and said, "Thanks for getting us out from hell. But I haven't been able to find my friend Stanislaw Zdanek."

Peter's heart squeezed at the mention of his brother's name. He tossed the thought aside. It would be too much of a coincidence to meet Stan here of all places – hundreds of miles away from home. "I'll check the camp hospital to make sure he'll be registered as Polish," Peter said and strode off, after assigning the newcomers to one of the barracks.

A new sense of urgency spurred him on and he rushed to the camp hospital in search of the missing prisoner, but the nurse, a prisoner himself, informed Peter they had received no patients with leg wounds in almost a week.

"Whomever you're looking for isn't here," he said solemnly.

"He's on the wounded list. He has to be here some-where," Peter insisted, taking another look at the sick men lying on beds.

"Did you check the dumpster?" the nurse asked.

"Dumpster?" Peter repeated.

"The tent where they take those who'll die anyways."

Peter felt a shiver running down his spine. A dumping

place for those not worth receiving medical assistance. The Nazis surely stopped at nothing. For a moment he pondered whether he should go to the tent. Until this moment he hadn't even known such a place existed, but he pulled himself together and trotted off to the farthest corner of the camp.

The sight and stench that greeted him made him gag. Outside the tent lay naked corpses piled up, waiting to be hauled away on carts to the nearby mass grave the next morning. Corpse disposal was a penal labor detail reserved for the Russians, but apparently the famished and enfeebled men hadn't been able to complete their work before darkness set in and they were locked into their barracks again.

Peter closed his eyes for a moment to send a prayer skyward and held a kerchief in front of his nose and mouth before he entered the tent. It took a while until his eyes adjusted to the dimness, the only light coming from the spotlights outside.

The skeletal, filthy men infested with lice didn't move to look at the visitor. They lay motionless on the ground, side by side, the dark shadow of death hovering over their heads. None of them would survive this night. Not in this tent.

He moved along the small path further into the room, with groaning and whimpering the only noises he could hear until the agonized scream of a man in pain reached his ears. At least his man was still well enough to scream. He followed the sound and soon squatted down next to a big man who wasn't as emaciated as the others.

"My leg…my leg…" the man whimpered in Polish.

Peter's chest constricted. He'd found the missing soldier. In the darkness he couldn't see the sick man's face. He murmured soothing words for the injured soldier. The man shifted at the sound of Peter's voice and Peter's heart plummeted as he recognized the pain-ravaged features that bore a faint resemblance to the boyish face of the brother he'd last seen five years ago. "Stan? Is this really you?"

"Piotr..." Stan whispered before his crazed eyes rolled back and he murmured incoherent words.

"God, Stan. Stan. Stan." Tears threatened to spill and Peter willed them down. Now wasn't the time to get emotional. If he wanted to save his brother he had to get him out of here immediately. "I'll get you into the hospital." Peter reached for his brother's arms, fear like he'd never known before racing through his mind, as he heaved him up and across his shoulders to carry him to the camp hospital.

CHAPTER 6: ANNA

At the Charité hospital in Berlin Anna was sitting at the desk jotting down information about the patients in her department when Professor Scherer, a handsome man in his fifties with salt-and-pepper hair, stopped by with more paperwork for her to look over.

"How are things going, Fräulein Klausen?" he asked politely. Since marrying a Slav was illegal according to the Nuremberg racial laws, she had married Peter in a clandestine Catholic ceremony performed by Pfarrer Bernau. For everyone except her immediate family, she still was a bachelorette.

"As good as can be given the situation. This war takes a toll on everyone." Anna looked up at the professor, who was her mentor and fatherly friend. One of the most renowned scientists in the Reich, Professor Scherer had contacts in the highest Nazi circles and rubbed elbows with Goebbels, Himmler and even Hitler himself. The head of the medicine and human genetics studies carried out at the prestigious

University Clinic Charité in Berlin, his one-of-a-kind work in the field of human biology catapulted his research light-years ahead of everyone else's.

When she'd first met him about a year ago, she'd admired both his brilliant mind and his impeccable, aristocratic manners. Becoming his protégée had been the shining point in her life – until darkness dimmed her admiration for him. While she still respected his scientific brilliance, she despised his lack of a conscience. He wasn't a fervent Nazi like so many others, but an opportunist who used his powerful connections exclusively to advance his own career.

Professor Scherer nodded and closed the door to the small nurse's office. When he returned, a worried look covered his face. "We will do the best we can, but this war might not end in a positive way for us."

Anna gasped. Saying Germany might lose the war was akin to sacrilege and could result in a conviction for *Wehrmachtzersetzung*, defamation of the Wehrmacht. Maybe she could manipulate his critical mood in her goal to find Peter. She carefully searched for words.

"Professor, I wonder what happened to your driver. Do you think he might be caught somewhere and needs our help?" Anna said with a shy smile.

Professor Scherer cast her an indulgent smile. "I know you fancied him, so I put out my feelers to investigate his whereabouts."

"Oh…" Anna felt the blood rushing to her cheeks. He had? And what had he found out? That Peter worked as a spy for the British and was in fact a Pole, not the German he claimed to be?

"Unfortunately I couldn't find out anything. Peter Wolf disappeared without a trace from the face of the earth after he took leave for personal affairs. I'm afraid that leaves only one conclusion..."

Anna nodded.

"...the Gestapo took him for whatever reason. These things happen." The professor pushed his glasses up on his nose and gave her a warning glance. "It is best if we never mention his name again, lest we get caught up in the net."

Anna nodded again. Maybe it was for the best that the professor thought Peter had been taken by the Gestapo. If someone found out what he'd really done and his current location, her own life would be hanging by a thin thread. A million ideas crossed her mind about how she could still enlist the professor's help to rescue Peter, but without his knowing her hidden motives.

"May I ask another question, Professor?"

"Sure, Fräulein Klausen."

"Wouldn't it be prudent to visit some of the camps?" He'd done this in the past, mostly to oversee the results of some of the horrific medical experiments performed on the hapless prisoners.

"Why would you suggest this?" The smile froze on his handsome features.

Anna struggled for words and cold sweat broke out on her forehead as she racked her brain for a believable excuse. "I...just thought...since there were news reports of recent outbreaks of typhus, and dysentery. We might need to do something...to prevent the disease from spreading to the civilians."

"That is a noble cause, but right now is not a good time

to be seen in the camps. If the worst happens and – God forbid – Germany does lose the war, it's best not to be associated with some of the things that have been happening there."

"I understand," Anna said with a mixture of awe and disgust. Professor Scherer had enough conscience to know the brutal treatment of the prisoners was wrong, but he still condoned it as long as it furthered his own career. He truly owned a brilliant – and shrewd – mind.

At the end of her shift attending to the never-ending influx of patients from the last nightly air raid, she took her bicycle and rode to her mother's place, which was now her home, too. On the way she had to stop several times and carry the bicycle across heaps of rubble and craters in the road, but it was still the fastest way to travel.

When she finally arrived home where Jan waited for her, sadness enveloped her heart over Peter. She hugged Jan, still amazed that at the age of twenty-two she'd suddenly become the stepmother of a twelve-year-old boy.

After everything he'd endured, the perceptive Jan picked up on her desolate mood and said, "Don't worry, Anna. My dad will come back. He found me once when everyone thought he was dead, and he will find me again."

CHAPTER 7: STAN

His world had dissolved into one of darkness and pain so intense he wished to die. His body was wracked with severe shaking even as he burned up from the blazing fever. In a moment of lucidity, he realized that his body was reacting to the bullet wound this way because it had become infected.

He'd not seen another waking human since the two soldiers had dumped him in this wasteland like a piece of human garbage. He closed his eyes, praying for his ordeal to be over soon, when a hallucination of his brother Peter manifested in his mind. Using it as the last straw that separated him from the other world, he clung to the sound of Peter's voice. In Stan's dream, his oldest brother peered down at him from above, calling his name and murmuring soothing words, before everything faded to black.

Stan woke with an unnerving feeling. When he felt movement, panic attacked him. He was not merely wriggling around in pain, but floating through the air. Despair settled in his chest as he concluded he must be headed to his eternal destiny. They must have come to toss him onto the pile of dead corpses. But why was he still in pain when he was dead?

"Hang on, Stan. Just hang on." His brother's voice came to him, but Stan couldn't find his own voice to call out for help.

Another voice spoke. The world around him got lighter and his body stopped moving. He tried to open his eyes, but his heavy lids prevented it. He sensed other people moving around him, and a scream of agony that must have been his own echoed in his ears. It felt like he was being torn limb from limb, until a sharp prick in his arm brought blessed relief.

The torment faded away and a numbness came over him. Stan's mind shut down and he floated into unconsciousness, taking comfort in the fact that wherever he was, it was a place devoid of the agony of the past days.

Stan rolled his fingers into his palm, scratching at his own skin. *If what they've told me was true and only the soul escapes to a better place, I'm not in the afterlife.* One by one his senses returned and he smelled a strange antiseptic odor. He heard hushed voices. Whimpering. He slowly opened his eyes and glanced around trying to figure out where he was. Scarred walls. Other men.

With great effort he turned his head and his eyes widened when he saw a familiar silhouette sitting beside his bed. It couldn't be true, or could it? The haggard man had bent his head into his hands. His uniform was torn and dirty, his dark blond hair and bearded face unkempt, but he'd know his oldest brother anywhere.

Stan opened his mouth and it took him two attempts before he finally found his voice. "Piotr?"

Peter's head popped up and relief filled his eyes. "Stan. You're awake."

"I'm thirsty."

Peter nodded and reached for a tin cup sitting on a nearby table. He held it to Stan's lips and despite the putrid smell, Stan drank the disgusting brown liquid, swallowing painfully. After downing the entire cup, the sawdust feeling in his throat dissolved and he felt a bit more human.

"Where are we?" Stan asked with a hoarse voice.

"Camp hospital, Stalag XIB in Fallingbostel near Hannover."

"I don't remember much. I was shot…a long train ride… dumped in a tent full of dying men." The talking had exhausted him and Stan slumped back against the pillow. Pillow? He noticed that he lay in a real bunk with a scratchy cloth beneath him and an even scratchier blanket covering his body.

"When I found you in that dump I thought for sure I'd lost you." Peter's voice betrayed his disturbing emotions.

"I believed I'd die there," Stan murmured, trying to tug the corners of his dry lips upward.

"Thank God I found you in time. You're not over the hump yet, but you'd better make it or I'll personally strangle you," Peter said with the same wicked grin he'd used on his younger brother when they were still children. Then he

41

produced a turnip and handed it to Stan with an apologetic shrug. "Here. That's all I've got."

Stan hated turnips nearly as much as he hated the Nazis, but what choice did he have? In his current condition he would have eaten worms and tree bark to fill his stomach. With the defiance of death he took the offered vegetable and nibbled at it. Between chews he said, "We thought you were dead. Where have you been all this time?"

"That's a long story. After the invasion I escaped to England and joined the British Army. I'll tell you about all of this later. Suffice to say I came into German captivity after the capitulation of the Home Army in the Warsaw Uprising."

"You were there?" Stan asked with a feeble voice, feeling the fever returning. The mention of Warsaw triggered bad memories and the grief about his murdered twin brother threatened to choke him. He whispered, "Jarek is dead."

Peter clasped Stan's hand and squeezed it tightly. "I heard."

"You heard?" Stan's head ached with the confusing information he was receiving.

"Yes, I met Agnieska in Warsaw and she told me."

So Agnieska is alive? The fog penetrating Stan's brain thickened, interrupted only by pangs of red-hot throbbing pain, and he barely heard Peter's next question about their sister. "You know of Katrina?"

"She escaped a Nazi raid and is hiding on a friend's farm."

"Thank God," Peter said, signs of relief showing in his face.

Stan remembered the escape at the last minute and how

he'd handed his sister and her boyfriend over to Bartosz. *Bartosz!* Just before another wave of agony engulfed him, he managed to say, "My friend, Bartosz. He was captured, too. Is he alive?"

Peter paused at the name and a slow grin crossed his face. "He is most definitely alive. In fact, he was the one who insisted I find you."

Stan closed his eyes, too weak and sick to continue the conversation. He groaned at the mounting pain and wished to return to the blessed darkness of unconsciousness.

"How's the pain?" Peter's voice came through the fog of agony.

"Climbing," Stan pressed through gritted teeth as he tried to ignore the sharp pain taking over and consuming his thinking.

"I'd get you a nurse to give you some morphine, if I could, but there's no such thing in here."

Stan clenched his fists in an attempt not to yell. Peter was alive. Bartosz was alive, and Agnieska, too. Maybe things weren't as bleak as they looked. Together they would persist and outlive those damn Nazis.

CHAPTER 8: ANNA

"Fräulein Klausen, do you have a minute?" Professor Scherer's question stopped her on her way out.

She inwardly groaned since she'd just finished her twelve-hour shift at the hospital. Every fiber in her body hurt from the backbreaking work of lifting, moving, and turning patients. All she wanted was to rush home and flop onto the couch, her feet up in the air.

But she mustered a smile and said, "Off course, Professor Scherer."

"Please accompany me to my office." He turned and led the way to the basement, where most of the doctors and scientists had taken up residence for security reasons. Ignoring her aching feet and throbbing back, she followed him and didn't even raise as much as an eyebrow when he closed and locked his office door before inviting her to sit at the small meeting table.

"Your remark about visiting the camps has been brewing in my mind for the last week. I think it's an excellent idea," he said, pouring them a glass of water each.

"What changed your mind, Professor?" Anna asked, not quite following.

"Can I trust you, Fräulein Klausen?"

Anna's ears perked up and her previously tired brain kicked into full gear, giving the professor its undivided attention. "You have my absolute loyalty, Professor. You are my boss and my mentor. I would never do anything to compromise you." It was true. In the current political climate he was one of the good fellows. Or at least one of the less evil ones. Either way, her fate was bound to his.

"I've been thinking about the time after the war ends." He took a sip from his water, pushing his glasses up on his nose the way he always did when he felt nervous or doubtful. Or both. He lowered his voice and continued, "I've come to the conclusion that a defeat of the Nazi regime is imminent."

"Defeat?" Anna all but gasped. Secretly she'd hoped, prayed and yearned for this to happen for the longest time, but hearing this verdict from one of the brightest men in Germany made it incredibly real.

"Unfortunately, yes. The news we receive from the propaganda ministry is meant to soothe the population, but what I hear from the generals is different. The Wehrmacht is attacked from East and West and reserves are depleted. The *Volkssturm* will only prolong the inevitable."

Anna nodded. The *Volkssturm* was Hitler's latest brilliant idea. She wondered whether anyone truly believed that sending untrained boys and old men into combat would turn the tide of the war.

"Or provide cannon fodder," she said and immediately wondered whether she'd revealed too much when she noticed the professor's surprised glance.

But he quickly composed himself and said, "When the Allies win they'll be out for revenge and mow down everyone considered a Nazi. They'll start with the obvious suspects. The Party leaders, the SS, SD, Gestapo…you name it. But I'm afraid they won't stop at that. In their blood thirst they'll go after everyone remotely involved with certain unfortunate things that happened."

Unfortunate things? You mean the extermination of an entire race in the death camps? Or the working-to-death of prisoners in the concentrations camps?

The professor pushed up his glasses again and gave her a long, sorrowful look. "You and I, we might both be exposed and dragged into the witch hunt, even though we've never actively participated in the injustices committed."

"We haven't?" Anna couldn't believe her ears.

Her mind drifted back to the all too fresh memory of the time she'd been tasked to research a tuberculosis vaccine. She'd later been horrified to learn that part of the experiment involved infecting imbecile children with the virus, even though no proof existed about the effectiveness of the vaccine.

"No, we haven't. None of us has ever killed a person or committed a similar atrocity."

The words caused her stomach to flip over. The blood drained from her face as the vicious abuse she'd suffered at Doctor Tretter's hands dragged her back in time to Ravensbrück.

"You should not worry, my dear Fräulein Klausen," the

professor said, mistaking her paleness for fear. "Because I have thought of a plan to position us in a more favorable situation."

Anna nodded, not really understanding his train of thought.

"So here's how your concern about the health issues in the camps comes into play. We'll dispense favors to those who can reciprocate should we need someone to vouch for us."

"I see." Anna didn't think she needed someone to vouch for her, but she could understand Professor Scherer's worries. He had a lot more to lose and he'd made his bed with the Nazis, which wouldn't serve him well after an Allied victory. "But how and where should we dispense favors?"

"Obviously to people who'll have something to say after the war. So we'll start with the prisoner camps where they keep officers."

"Doing what?" Anna asked, her heart hammering as she immediately thought of seeing Peter again.

"We're going there to vaccinate the prisoners against typhus."

"But we don't have enough serum to vaccinate hundreds of thousands of prisoners," Anna objected.

"That is true. Therefore we will only vaccinate the officers, but they will recognize our goodwill and make sure my name will be mentioned as someone who has helped them alleviate their dire conditions."

Anna fluctuated between being appalled at the professor's deliberate activities to save his own skin and admiration for his brilliant plan. It would work, she was sure of it.

What unfortunate prisoner wouldn't remember the man who came to offer even a modest relief? Could she even condemn the professor for wanting to protect his future? Was it bad to do the right thing, if it was done for the wrong reasons?

She decided to put all scruples aside and use Professor Scherer's plan of redemption to further her own ends and find a way to get Peter out of captivity.

"That is an excellent idea, Professor. We will do some good for those pour souls."

"I always intended my research to benefit all mankind, but the political climate in Germany didn't allow for this," he said with a grave voice. Then he clapped his hands and said with much more enthusiasm, "We'll start tomorrow morning. Our first visit will be the *Reservelazarett V* here in Berlin. Meet me there at eight." The Reservelazarett was a temporary hospital that usually hosted wounded Wehrmacht soldiers, but this one also treated a few dozen enemy officers.

"Yes, Professor. Good night." Anna stood and left the office to return home.

Her sister Ursula greeted her with baby Eveline in her arms. "You look tired."

"I am. We receive more patients every day and two of the nurses didn't show up this morning. Nobody knows their whereabouts."

Ursula nodded. She didn't need to say a word for Anna to understand her thoughts. *Probably killed in the last air raid.*

"Shush, Evie," Ursula said and put her finger into the baby's mouth to soothe her.

"Can I hold her?"

"Sure." Ursula handed over the baby and disappeared into the kitchen to return a few moments later with two cups of steaming tea. The scent of lemon balm reviving Anna's energy.

"Thanks." Anna settled onto the couch with the baby on her lap, putting her feet up and swallowing the hot, slightly acidic liquid. It trickled down her throat all the way into her stomach and warmed her from inside. "Professor Scherer wants to commend himself to the Allies and plans a vaccination campaign in one of the Reservelazaretts."

"That doesn't make much sense, does it?" Ursula said, rising an eyebrow.

"Oh, it does. He'll vaccinate enemy officers, hoping they'll survive the war and vouch for him to whomever has the say after all of this is over."

"Wow. So even he is convinced the Allies will win?"

"He considers it a very real possibility and is planning ahead to secure his future." Anna paused for a moment, before she continued, "If I could convince him to visit Fallingbostel…"

Ursula's eyes widened and she put down her cup with a thud on the small couch table. "You're not still thinking about seeing Peter?"

"I am." Anna pushed out her lower lip, awaiting a stern sermon from her older sister.

"Do you know how dangerous this is? And foolish? If the Gestapo finds out who Peter really is, we'll all be dead."

"Nobody will find out."

Ursula rolled her eyes, opening her mouth to dive into another monologue, but Anna stopped her with a severe glare.

"I have to do this. And you know it. If there's even the slightest chance to rescue Peter and–"

"You crazy woman. Do you really think freeing Peter is even a possibility? It's not like you can just go in and walk out with him."

Anna clung to the warm baby in her arms, pushing all doubts aside. "It has worked with Lotte…"

"It did," Ursula said, shoving Anna's legs aside to settle beside her on the couch. "But at what price? Do you really want to go through this again?"

Anna shivered at the memory of the worst time in her life. "I'll think of a better plan this time. Once he's out of there he can resume his German identity."

"Don't get your hopes up; the chances that you'll actually be able to get Peter out and both of you live to tell the tale are next to zero." Ursula put her arm across Anna's shoulders and added, "But if you need my help, you know where to find me."

CHAPTER 9: ANNA

Anna stood in front of the Reservelazarett. Wisps of mist hung in the cold air of this November morning. The colorful leaves of the chestnut trees had long fallen to the ground and blown away to mix with with the rubble from the bombed out buildings.

The hospital was located in a school building. Education wasn't a priority anymore and most of the schools hadn't reopened after the summer break. Teachers were fighting at the front or working in ammunition factories. The students who hadn't been sent away to the countryside with the *Kinderlandverschickung* were collecting scrap metal or used paper instead of learning.

Everything and everyone for the war effort. She scoffed. When would this craziness end? And what would happen then? She didn't delude herself that things would be all sunshine and roses, but she also hoped things wouldn't get any worse.

Several minutes later, Professor Scherer's Mercedes

limousine arrived along with his new driver Hans Gerber. She disliked Hans, and not just because he'd replaced her beloved Peter, but mostly because she didn't trust him. He was one of the most fervent Nazis she'd met in her life, a member of the SS proudly representing Hitler's ideals.

"Good morning, Schwester Anna," he said, using her job title to address her.

"Good morning, Hans." She forced a pleasant smile on her face, ignoring the shivers on her back she always felt in his presence.

He opened the back door of the Mercedes and helped Professor Scherer from the car.

"Good morning, Fräulein Klausen, punctual as always. Shall we go?" The professor fell in step beside her, leaving Hans carrying the heavy box with the medical supplies.

Since the professor had phoned in the day before, the head doctor of the small hospital eagerly awaited them, impressed at receiving a visit by the well-known scientist.

"It's such an honor to receive you here. Although," the doctor cast his eyes downward and rubbed his hands, "I have to warn you that the conditions in the prisoner ward are not up to medical standards. We never receive enough materials, and priority is given to the Wehrmacht soldiers."

Professor Scherer gave him a benevolent smile and Anna admired once again the ease with which he won over people and made them feel appreciated. "That's the exact reason why my assistant, Fräulein Klausen, and I have come here. We won't be able to work a miracle, but we brought enough serum to vaccinate fifty officers against typhus."

The doctor's eyes lit up. "You cannot imagine how much I appreciate this. An outbreak of this disease in the prisoner ward would undoubtedly spread into the main section and possibly into the civil population."

With the head doctor in tow, Anna and Professor Scherer entered the prisoner ward. A shudder racked her body. As a practicing nurse at the Charité, she saw plenty of gore and pus, but she hadn't expected the desolate condition of the ward. It reminded her of the sick bay at the Ravensbrück concentration camp, just more crowded.

A slew of even more ghastly memories from her time working at the concentration camp attacked her and she swayed. Taking a calming breath, the putrid stench burnt a blaze deep down into her stomach. She closed her eyes, pulling herself together. Here, nothing could happen to her. Doctor Tretter was dead. Killed with her own hands.

The head doctor introduced them and announced the plan to vaccinate the officers against typhus. He then accompanied Professor Scherer as they conversed with the highest-ranking officers amongst them, obviously making sure they remembered the name and face of their benefactor.

Anna forced a smile to her face and opened her medical bag. "Who wants to be first? It won't hurt."

"Me," a handsome man answered in a thick accent she barely understood. Judging by his uniform he was American. "A beautiful lady like you can prick me all she wants."

Her smile turned from forced to genuine. Despite their dire situation these lads hadn't lost their good humor. And getting a good look at them from close up, they looked just like the Wehrmacht soldiers she'd treated. Young men – humans – who wanted nothing more than to stay alive and return home to their families.

She put a patch on the puncture in his skin and said, "Next one, please." Soon, the walking wounded formed a queue to be treated by the peachy nurse.

"Will you marry me when the war is over, beautiful lady?" another man asked.

Anna shook her head and smiled. "As much as I'd love to, I'm afraid my fiancé would object."

"Lucky bastard," the man answered and vacated his place for the next patient.

"Actually, I'm the lucky one," she murmured, unaware that an older officer had already taken the seat across from hers. He looked straight into her eyes and she couldn't keep a single tear from slipping down her cheek.

"I'll pray that he returns to your side safely," he said, baring his arm for her to put the needle in.

"Thank you." *He's a prisoner of war, just like you,* she wanted to add, but couldn't risk being exposed.

When she'd vaccinated everyone in the queue, she stored the supplies in her medical bag and ventured to inspect those that couldn't walk. She wouldn't be able to administer them the serum, because the vaccine would probably kill them in their weakened condition, but perhaps she could alleviate their suffering in other ways.

She organized a glass of water, changed a dressing here and cleaned a wound there, when she came upon a half-conscious man with crazed eyes, whimpering in pain. It squeezed her heart to look at him, because she could see the death in his eyes. There was neither help nor hope for the young fellow.

Anna rummaged in her bag and found what she was

looking for. The older officer she'd given the typhus vaccine earlier had caught up with her, giving her a knowing glance.

"I'm sorry for your comrade," she said and handed him the ampule of morphine. "When it gets worse, give him this."

"God bless you, nurse."

~

"Our visit went well," Professor Scherer said, sitting beside her in the back of his limousine, as they headed for the Charité.

"Those poor men were really grateful," Anna said, remembering how the men had promised her fortunes and eternal gratitude for the smallest deeds of humanity.

"It was well beyond my expectations, and we should make these visits a regular routine."

Anna nodded and gave voice to the idea that had been running around in her brain since their arrival at the hospital. "While I think it is necessary to vaccinate everyone, we don't have enough serum to do so. Perhaps we should concentrate our efforts on the non-wounded officers that have better chances at survival?"

The professor looked at her for a long minute. "That is an excellent idea. Limited resources have to be distributed to where they have the highest impact." His eyes flickered for a short moment. "While this may be unfortunate or even cruel for the individual, it is for the best of society as a whole. Since I'll be caught up in meetings for the next few days, may I put this into your hands?"

"It would be my pleasure," Anna said, her heart hammering staccato in her throat.

"Chose the best-suited prisoner camp and make the arrangements for us to visit next week through my secretary. Remember we want to reach as many nationalities as possible."

"I'll get right on it." Anna wanted to scream with joy. Now she had the perfect excuse to see Peter.

CHAPTER 10: PETER

Two weeks later at the prison camp Fallingbostel

Word got out that an official committee would arrive for inspection, and everyone was prompted to leave the barracks spick and span.

"It's a waste of time and energy," Peter growled at the enthusiasm of his co-prisoners.

"Come on. It could even be the International Red Cross and they might bring packages from home," Bartosz said on a hopeful note.

"Well, we can hope," Peter agreed and continued sweeping the floor.

It was more probable that some high-ranking Nazis wanted to visit with the sole intent of patting themselves on the back. Back in the days with Professor Scherer, he'd been part of many such official committees, which had never improved the conditions for the prisoners. On the contrary, most of the times, some ridiculous work quotas had been instigated due to the *lazy* behavior the famished prisoners displayed. Cleaning up the camp for whoever these visitors were would actually go against their own interests.

But he knew all too well that he didn't have a choice. *Do what the guard says or face the consequences.* So he finished sweeping and stripped naked to join the queue of men waiting patiently to take a bath in one of the large wooden pails.

He shivered in the cold December air and when it was his turn he immersed himself in the murky liquid, ignoring the pungent smell of the delousing agent. The freezing water took his breath away and numbed his already cold limbs. He quickly washed himself with his hands and let a comrade scratch his back, before he jumped outside to dry himself off with his kerchief.

Despite the iciness in his bones, he smiled. For a few days he wouldn't have to worry about itching louse bites. Even if the important visitors didn't improve matters in any other way, the delousing bath was well worth the extra effort.

Then he joined the other barracks seniors to meet with the camp commandant and receive further instructions for the upcoming official visit. Peter didn't pay much attention to the usual slogans, until the commandant said, "The visiting party has suggested distributing typhus vaccines to two hundred prisoners…"

Wow! Now that was a game changer. Two hundred wasn't nearly enough, obviously, but it could help keep the deadly disease at bay. Typhus was one of the biggest problems in any camp, and the insidious disease had taken many lives in Fallingbostel for weeks. It was only a matter of time before it turned into a full-blown epidemic and threatened to wipe out a big percentage of the prisoners.

"...We are fortunate that someone as renowned in the field of bacteriology as Professor Scherer has selected this camp as a test case for his immunization program..."

Peter didn't understand the rest of the commandant's words due to the heavy rushing of blood to his ears. *Professor Scherer of all persons!* Peter wanted to shrink to Tom Thumb size and stay that way until the official visit ended. It was dreadful to imagine what would happen if the professor recognized him, as he was bound to. A fast death would be the best-case scenario, but ending up in one of the Gestapo's torture chambers was much more likely if anyone ever found out that Peter Wolf and Piotr Zdanek were the same person...and had been spying for the British.

"Those who aren't on a work party will line up in front of their barracks and wait for our visitors. I expect you to make the best possible impression...or you will regret it." The commandant dismissed the barracks seniors with a wave of his hand.

Peter left the office with the other men, his mind swirling frantically to devise a plan to keep from being discovered. He needed to hide, and fast. On returning to his own barracks, he pulled Bartosz aside.

"You need to cover for me," Peter said.

Bartosz, a man of few words, eyed him for a long time and said, "Sure. What do you need me to do?"

"Assume my position as barracks senior and make sure everything goes off without a hiccup."

Bartosz raised a brow.

"If the visitor sees me, not only is my life at stake, but possibly all of yours as well."

"Understood. Where will you go?"

"I don't know yet, but I'll find someplace to hunker down until they leave."

Bartosz followed Peter inside, where Peter explained to the men about the vaccinations and that Bartosz would fill in for him as barracks senior, because he had been assigned to the sick bay. As the lie fell easily from his lips, Peter knew his men wouldn't question him, and they never went near the sick bay if they weren't forced to.

Actually the sick bay was a good place to hide. The doctors wouldn't waste the precious serum on dying men, and he could chat with Stan for a while. Thoughts of his brother brought a deep frown to his forehead. Stan still couldn't get up and was weakening by the day. He was slowly dying, despite the care he'd been given.

Minutes later Peter snuck into the sick bay, his eyes adjusting to the dim light inside.

"Piotr?" Stan raised his hand in an inviting gesture.

"Shush. Nobody can know I was here."

"What?" Stan's voice was weak, and it hurt Peter's soul to see his temperamental, strong-willed and vibrant younger brother lying within the clutches of death.

"Someone from my past is coming to the camp. He'll be sure to recognize me if he sees me, but he believes I'm a loyal Nazi. I can't let him find me." Peter ran a hand through his freshly cropped hair and glanced around. Some of the other injured men stirred. Maybe his plan wasn't as bullet-proof as he'd thought. But where else could he hide? "I can't stay here. It's too dangerous."

"'The bone yard," Stan said and after noticing the confused glance on Peter's face added, "The tent where you found me, where they take the hopeless cases and leave them to die."

Peter gagged at the memory and every fiber in his body revolted at the notion of returning to that ghastly place, but he knew Stan was right. It was the one place in the camp where he would be safe from discovery. He pushed a piece of bread into Stan's hand and said, "You owe me. Take care."

For a tiny moment Stan's eyes flickered with his usual energy as he answered, "Don't die on me, brother."

Peter slipped through the doorway and out the back of the building. He made it to Hell's waiting room without encountering anyone. Nobody would come here until morning when the penal party had to retrieve the corpses and transport them to the burial pit.

He entered the dimly lit tent and pulled a kerchief over his mouth and nose to keep out the stench of death that seemed to permeate the very walls. His eyes glued to the entrance, he slumped on the floor with nothing to do but wait.

It would be a horrendous wait.

Peter thought about everything he'd left behind in Berlin, including his beautiful Anna. He missed her so much and wished he could at least let her know that he was still alive. Other prisoners had been allowed to write home, but how should he explain that his secret wife lived in Berlin and was German?

Meeting her again would have to wait until after the war. The news brought by newcomers promised that it wouldn't take much longer. And Peter was determined to survive this war, but first, he had to survive the rest of this day.

CHAPTER 11: ANNA

Anna sat in the back of the Mercedes limousine with Professor Scherer, the trunk loaded with a large supply of vaccines and other materials from the research center at the Charité. Officially all research had been stopped and resources transferred to the hospital area of the clinic, but the professor had powerful connections. Once again Anna was left with her jaw hanging at the ease with which he'd been able to assign two laboratory technicians to help her growing bacteria cultures for the serum. She herself had been absolved from her nurse duties and transferred once again to the biology institute.

Hans mumbled, disgusted about the bad shape of the roads to Fallingbostel, claiming the Jews had done this to Germany. Anna pursed her lips at the ridiculous yet hateful remarks this dyed-in-the-wool Nazi was making. She bit the inside of her cheek to hold back the words that wanted to spill forth.

She glanced at the professor, who was reading some

scientific material and either didn't hear Hans' words or simply ignored them. She shrugged. Professor Scherer might be the biggest opportunist on earth, but he wasn't cruel and spiteful like his driver.

In fact, she'd never heard him say a bad word about the Jews. Even one of his former friends was a Jew, the publisher Louis Ullstein, who'd emigrated a decade ago after selling his mansion to the professor.

Anna leaned back into the leather seat, doing her best to calm her racing heart and her sweating palms. Soon she'd see Peter again. She'd still not come up with a plan to get him out of the camp, but she trusted that her mind would come up with something once she'd been able to take a closer look at the location. Hans continued to spill his vitriol, but she tuned out his voice and closed her eyes to relish her dreams about a happy reunion with Peter.

After a long yet pleasant drive with only a short stop to eat some lunch, they arrived at Fallingbostel in the early afternoon. As soon as the Mercedes pulled up in front of the gate, two Wehrmacht guards rushed out and ushered them to the commandant's quarters a few hundred yards from the camp.

"Professor Scherer, what an honor to have you here," the commandant said.

"Kommandant Greiner, it's my pleasure," the professor said, shaking hands, before he introduced Anna as his assistant.

"A pleasure to meet you, Fräulein Klausen." A frown crossed Kommandant Greiner's forehead. "I will assign two guards for your security. These foreigners can't be trusted..."

"I don't think that will be necessary, Kommandant," Anna protested. She'd rather go without two watchdogs by her side.

"No, I insist. You are under my protection and I will ensure your security during your stay at the camp."

"Well then, thank you." She cast him a smile, well aware that at this point any resistance would have been futile.

Kommandant Greiner accompanied them on a tour through the camp, including one of the barracks. Anna's eyes grew bigger and bigger. She'd expected to find appalling conditions similar to what she'd seen in the women's camp in Ravensbrück, but here everything was scrubbed clean and flashed in the December sunshine. The prisoners, while emaciated, wore clean uniforms, were freshly shaven and bathed and didn't seem to be pestered with lice.

Professor Scherer asked the officers and barracks seniors to form a line and held a lengthy speech about the virtues of morality, especially in times of war. He then continued to stress that he'd convinced the Ministry of Health to allow him to vaccinate prisoners of war to prevent a major humanitarian disaster.

Anna observed with amazement how the hostile expressions on the prisoners' faces turned to skepticism and finally to agreement. On the professor's wink, she ordered her two watchdogs to scrounge a table and two chairs and opened her medical suitcase to start administering the vaccines the same way she'd done at the Reservelazarett.

Her boss engaged some of the higher-ranking officers in conversation, obviously making sure they would remember the name and face of their benefactor. Anna, though, was more interested in finding a certain man. Since he was an officer, too, he should have been in the group.

Hours later her serum had run out with still no sight of him. Her heart squeezed painfully.

What if he is dead? No, you can't think like that. He's fine. He must be fine.

Then it hit her between the eyes and she gasped, attracting the glances of some of the nearby prisoners. He must be hiding, afraid the professor might recognize him! How stupid of her not to consider this aspect. Hot and cold waves shot up and down her spine, making breathing difficult, as she realized the danger she'd exposed him to. If Professor Scherer had seen and recognized Peter…the blood drained from her head and a dizzy feeling claimed her.

"Excuse me, I need to get some air," she hissed and fanned herself with a sheet of paper. She jumped up, pushing the loaded syringe into the hands of one of the stupefied guards, and rushed off.

The prisoners opened their ranks to make space for her, each one looking more confused than the next, but nobody dared to talk to her. She walked a minute or two, until she stopped in front of barracks with a huge "P" for Polish painted on it.

New hope filled her soul. She entered the dimly lit structure and asked, "Does anyone know a man called Piotr Zdanek?"

The two men inside eyed her suspiciously and looked away, pretending not to understand or not to know. But she'd seen the glimmer of recognition in their eyes and could tell they knew him. So he wasn't dead.

A moment later, one of the guards bolted into the barracks, ready to take it up with whoever was in there.

"What the hell are you doing, woman? This is not a pony farm; these men are dangerous. Enemies." As he yelled, he pointed an accusing finger at her.

"I'm sorry," Anna turned around to bedazzle the elderly *Landesschütze* with her brightest smile. "I had an anxiety attack back there. Thank you for coming to my rescue."

She stepped toward him and graciously offered him her arm to lead her outside. The bright sun reflecting on remnants of snow patches blinded her and she used her hand to shield her eyes, berating herself for her rash behavior. Nobody could know that she knew Peter. Back at her makeshift medical station, she packed her bag and looked for her boss.

"If you're looking for Professor Scherer, he's at the commandant's office, they asked not to be disturbed," one of her guards said.

"Thank you. I…" A plan formed in her mind. "…will need to see the sick bay, would you please guide me there," she said, as if it were the most normal thing in the world.

"But…Fräulein, that wasn't…"

"Look." She glared at him, before she softened and cast him a smile. "I'm sorry if you weren't instructed on the details of our visit, but it's imperative that I visit the sick bay. So if you have doubts, we can pass by the office and ask Kommandant Greiner."

Discomfort etched itself into the man's expression and he shook his head. "That won't be necessary, Fräulein. I'll show you the way."

The sick bay looked a lot more like she'd expected, and

suspicion entered her brain. Could it be that the camp had been given a quick makeover for the official guests? She pushed the thought aside, for now her only concern was to find Peter.

The guard opened the door for her and a putrid stench attacked her nostrils. Definitely comparable to Ravensbrück. A gagging noise reached her ear and she turned around to see her watchdog pale. Some people didn't have the stomach for gore and pus.

"Would you rather wait outside?" she asked with her sweetest voice.

"I should stay at your side," he said, swallowing hard.

"I'm sure I can manage alone. Look at these men, they aren't even able to raise a hand. And I promise to yell if anyone bothers me. You stay at the door and wait."

He seemed to be torn between his duty and the queasy stomach the hospital barracks caused him, and Anna played her trump. "Nobody has to know. I certainly won't tell anyone."

A grateful expression flickered across his face and he nodded. "I'll be right outside."

The door clicked shut behind him and a sigh of relief escaped her. Maybe one of the wounded soldiers would talk. As she'd expected, there weren't any doctors or nurses in the so-called hospital. She knew that in most camps the prisoners themselves staffed the hospitals and attended the patients only after their other chores. Today they would be in the gathering place to make a good impression on the visitors.

Anna walked along a narrow aisle with bunks on both sides. Most of the bunks were filled with two or three men, covered with filthy blankets. *Dear God, have those people never heard about hygiene and sanitary conditions?*

She distributed water from her bottle and wiped away puke and blood, but that was about all she could do for them. At the end of the building she heard a pained groan and stepped toward the man. When she saw his face, she struggled to hold in an appalled gasp.

The man looked so much like Peter, she had to take a second look. This man's hair was blonder, his face more square-jawed and he seemed younger, but the similarity was striking. She stepped forward, her eyes fixated on his baby-blues.

"Why are you staring at me? Never seen a dying man?" Stan said gruffly.

Anna gave him an empathetic smile. "You're not dying yet. Please forgive me, but you look so much like someone I know...someone I was hoping to see while I was here..."

Stan narrowed his gaze and asked, "What's this some-one's name?"

"Piotr Zdanek."

He gave a slight shake of his head. "Not me."

"So who are you?"

Stan eyed her suspiciously, but finally answered her, probably because he knew she could find out anyways. "Stanislaw Zdanek."

Anna gasped again and searched his face. "Stan? One of the twins?"

"How do you know?"

"Because Peter...Piotr..." She wondered how much Stan knew about her and Peter and whether it was safe to tell him they were secretly married. "...because we're in love."

Now it was Stan's turn to gasp.

"You know where he is? I need to find him. Please."

His tortured eyes narrowed. "Hold on a minute, lady. How do I know you're really a friend?" Stan hissed the question, the effort of talking so much making him sweat.

Anna cleaned his forehead with her kerchief, while her brain worked overtime. How could she convince the suspicious man that she didn't pose a threat for Peter?

"Janusz lives with me in Berlin," she offered for proof.

Stan scoffed. "Nice try. Not possible."

"Please, you have to believe me," Anna begged. "I planned this entire visit just to find him. Ask me anything. I'm sure I can dispel your doubts."

Stan glared at her, seemingly fighting with himself, but he finally relented and said, "What was the name of Janusz's pet dog?"

Pet dog? Neither Peter nor Jan had ever mentioned a dog. She gazed at Stan and recognized the twitching of his lip, the same way Peter's did when he teased her. "He never had a dog."

If Stan seemed surprised, he didn't show it. "We have another brother. What's his name?"

"Jarek."

"Who's older, Jarek or me?"

"You're twins," she said. "I don't know who's older, but I know that you're the quick-tempered, stubborn one always willing to solve a problem with your fists, while Jarek's the one who keeps you grounded."

"Was."

"Was?" Anna stared at him for a moment until the pain

on his face brought the revelation. "I'm sorry for the loss of your brother."

"I believe you," Stan said after a while. "Piotr is hiding in the bone yard."

"The bone yard? Where is this?"

"No idea. I was unconscious when Piotr carried me out of there."

The pallor on Stan's face intensified with the effort and she put a hand on his shoulder. "I'll find him. What happened to you?"

"Bullet in the leg. Got infected."

Anna reached out and felt for his pulse, concerned with the weakness. "Did they give you something?"

"They don't waste medicine on prisoners who'll die anyway."

"Don't talk like that. I'll get you help." Anna forced a confident smile on her face, but she feared for the worst. The infection he'd contracted was serious.

He sneered, clearly not believing that there was still help for him.

She slipped from the building into the dusk that cast a golden light onto the camp and took a deep breath of fresh winter air. Right in this moment, the place looked serene and peaceful. But she knew she had to hurry up if she wanted to find Peter. Professor Scherer expected her in one hour from now to return to Berlin.

"Finished, Fräulein?" The guard stepped toward her, apparently eager to return to the office area.

Shoot. She'd completely forgotten about him.

"Almost, but I need to have a look at the bone yard. Can

71

you take me there?" The shock on his face almost made her laugh.

"N…n….nobody ever goes there, except for the penal work parties. Y…y…you shouldn't go there." He inched backwards, holding tight onto his rifle.

"Believe me, I hate this as much as you do, but I became aware of an awful breach of hygiene that could endanger the life of everyone in this camp, including the guards. It could even spread to the civilian population of the town." Seeing that he wasn't convinced, she asked, "What's your name?"

"Jochen Kaufmann."

"Well, Herr Kaufmann, wouldn't Kommandant Greiner be pleased if you were the one to save thousands of German citizens from dying of an epidemic?" She gave him an encouraging smile.

"I guess…"

"You might even receive a promotion."

His eyes lit up. "You think so?"

"Certainly. Take me there and keep watch. It's best if no one except me goes inside, because of the danger of contagion."

"We need to hurry, since there's no light back there," he said and marched off, Anna falling in step with him.

It took them almost ten minutes to reach the farthest corner of the camp, and then she stood in front of the shabbiest tent-like structure she'd ever seen in her life. Despite the low temperature, the stench from rotting corpses was repulsive.

She pulled a face mask across mouth and nose, before she entered saying, "I'll be right back."

Inside it was almost dark, with corpses and half-dead people piled up higher than her own height. A shiver racked her body. In the twilight she believed she saw the dancing shadows of tortured souls coming to haunt the living. She shook her head. Dead people couldn't harm her. It was the living she should be afraid off.

To dispel the fear, she hummed a happy melody, until one of the shadows stepped out from the twilight and stopped in front of her.

She opened her mouth to scream, but no sound came out.

CHAPTER 12: ANNA

Panic rose in her body, escalating as a big, bony hand covered her face and warm breath hit the skin on her cheek. The blood rushed in her ears so loud, she almost didn't hear the whispered voice.

"Anna. Shush. Don't scream."

Peter! He was here! She'd found him. Her heart did a double flip and she nodded her understanding. The hand slipped from her mouth, taking the face mask with it, and two strong hands turned her around and pressed her against his chest. She gasped in shock, because the skeletal body didn't resemble the husband who'd left six months ago.

"Anna. Is it really you? Sweetheart. My darling." He showered her with breathless kisses between murmured words of endearment.

"You're here. I found you," she murmured against his lips, before his demanding kiss silenced every thought in her mind and she gave herself over to the sensation. When they came up for air, she said, "Oh, God, Peter. When I didn't see you amongst the other prisoners, I was so afraid that I'd come too late."

"Bad weeds grow tall." His crooked grin couldn't hide the emotion in his damp eyes. He hugged her close again, devouring her mouth in a passionate kiss. "I've dreamed of you every single day...I can't believe you're here."

"In the flesh." Anna tried to lighten the mood even as tears ran down her face. The stolen seconds ticked by and she remembered that she didn't have much time. "I saw your brother Stan...he told me where you were."

Peter's jaw tightened. "Stan's not doing well."

"No wonder, in theses conditions. He's fighting off an infection," Anna whispered, soaking up the warmth of being in Peter's arms.

"Yeah, he hasn't improved since they removed the bullet and stitched him up."

Anna nodded. "I...have a plan to get you out of here." It wasn't actually a plan, but more a straw she hung on to. "Stay put. I'll return."

A sound outside the door brought Anna and Peter abruptly apart. Peter disappeared into the shadows just in time when a beam of light illuminated the spot where he'd been standing seconds earlier.

"Landesschüzte Kaufmann," Anna said, slightly panicked.

"Professor Scherer is asking for you," the guard said, standing in the entrance.

"I'm just finishing up. Your superior will be pleased with you," she said.

The guard nodded once and hurried away from the bone

yard in such haste, Anna had difficulty keeping up with his pace.

CHAPTER 13: PETER

He forced himself to wait several minutes before leaving his hiding place. On the way back he passed the hospital barracks and decided to pay Stan another visit. Perhaps to make sure his brother was alright, or to distract himself from worrying about Anna and her plan to get him out of here.

It wasn't that he didn't want to escape, but he loathed endangering her by doing so. Since she hadn't elaborated, he had no idea what kind of crazy plan she'd cooked up.

Stan was awake when Peter slipped into the room, and by the glare in his eyes Peter could tell that he was about to receive a dressing down from his younger brother.

"The nurse. Who is she?" Stan whispered angrily.

Peter swallowed and sat on the bunk. "Her name is Anna and I met her in Berlin while working for the professor." Stan already knew that Peter had been placed by the British into the position of Professor Scherer's driver. It had been an invaluable source of information, because the professor socialized with the who's who of the Nazis and after a few drinks the men often said things they usually wouldn't.

"Is she your mistress?" Stan glared at his brother, demanding an explanation.

Peter shook his head at the vehemence in his brother's voice. "Don't you ever talk about her like that again. I love her."

"You love her? A German!" Stan sneered. "How could you?"

Peter balled his hands into fists. Stan was his brother, and he was gravely sick, but that didn't give him the right to question Peter's feelings. "She's my wife and you'd better respect her."

Peter watched his brother's eyes flare up with rage and prepared himself for one of Stan's famous tirades, but he only clenched his jaw several times before his head fell back on the bunk. "You married a....a...German! You must be nuts," Stan whispered furiously, his energy waning.

"So how is this different from our sister Katrina falling in love with a German soldier?" Peter couldn't help but remark pointedly.

"Believe me, I did my best to keep them apart," Stan said, his breath coming in huffs and his eyelids drooping. "At least Richard helped to rescue your son from the ghetto."

"See, Anna is doing the same. She told me she's strategizing to get me out of here." The moment the words left his mouth, Peter realized how insensible they sounded.

Stan's eyes widened and he shoved himself up the side of the bed, but his struggles and his weakness were not a good combination and he fell forward before Peter could grab him. Stan collapsed on the floor next to the bed, a scream of pain tearing from his lips.

"Stan!" Peter took his brother by the shoulders and pulled him up. He kept tugging until Stan was leaning over the bed once more. "What were you thinking?"

"Nothing. I'm not thinking. Ever." Stan turned his head and gave Peter a bleak stare. "My mind is a black hole ever since Jarek died. We've been together every single day of our lives and now he's gone." Stan's voice broke and his body slumped onto the bed like a sack of flour. Peter knew that Jarek and Stan had shared a bond that only other twins could dream of understanding.

"I wish I had died before you found me. At least I wouldn't be lonely anymore," Stan sobbed.

Peter shook his head. "Don't say that," he whispered in his brother's ear. "Don't ever say that."

"Why not?" Stan asked, levering himself back up onto the bed, wincing with each movement. "It's the truth. When you leave, there will be no one left with me…" Stan's voice trailed off and his eyes rolled back in his head.

Concerned, Peter scanned the prone body lying on the bed, cursing when he saw the telltale red stain spreading out beneath his thighs. He rushed outside and called for help. Guilt swamped him when one of the prisoners who acted as doctor entered the barracks.

"He's losing too much blood," the man announced, even as he inspected the wound that had torn open from the fall.

"Stitch him up. Do something," Peter urged him.

"I'm afraid he'll die. The only option would be giving him a blood transfusion, but we don't have the means here."

The older Pole gave Peter a compassionate glance. "There's really nothing I can do."

Peter pounded his fist against the wall, not willing to give up. He'd seen one of those strange transfusion devices before. It was a T-shaped syringe with a rubber hose attached to it on both sides. Obviously they didn't have one in the camp. That kind of modern medical equipment was reserved for the Germans.

His mind went into a frenzy. *Anna.* What if she had one in her medical suitcase? She would help him. He had to find her. For a moment he hesitated and pondered the consequences. If he ran into Professor Scherer...

"Would you ask the nurse who's here to help us?" he asked the doctor. "She might have a transfusion syringe."

The older man gave him a confused stare, "What makes you think the Nazi nurse will help a Polish prisoner?

Peter cringed at the contemptuous tone, but kept an expressionless face. "She came here for vaccinations...I believe she has a good heart."

"A Nazi and a good heart? You should hear yourself talking this nonsense. Even if she has a transfusion syringe, who will donate the blood?"

"Me," Peter said, squaring his shoulders. He'd do anything to save his younger brother.

"We'd have to run tests on your blood type and his, otherwise the danger is too great, and..."

Before the man could voice more objections, Peter interrupted him, "Please. This man is my brother. We share the same blood type. You have to save him."

The doctor raised his brows and then nodded. "Alright. I will ask the nurse. You stay and put pressure on his wound."

With these words the doctor took off for the commandant's office and left a very worried Peter behind.

"You're not going to die on me, Stan," he said, but his brother had faded into unconsciousness and couldn't hear him.

CHAPTER 14: ANNA

"Good, you're back," Professor Scherer said. "How did the immunizations go?"

"Perfect. The prisoners behaved extremely well. I must say, your camp is one of the best-organized ones I've seen, Kommandant Greiner," she said with a smile, her thoughts in full gear on who would be best to propose her plan.

"I do what I can," the commandant said, his face gleaming with pride. "It's important to keep the prisoners at bay or you risk outbreaks of chaos and disorder."

"The success of our campaign is in large part due to your excellent help," Professor Scherer said and then addressed Anna, "Kommandant Greiner invited me to join him for dinner tonight."

Anna held her breath; entertaining a bunch of Nazis was the last thing she wanted to do. But she shouldn't have worried, because he added, "Of course, I will arrange for my driver to return you home, since I will be staying at least two more days and also meeting up with the commandant from the nearby camp in Bergen-Belsen."

Her heart leapt with joy and she quickly asked, "May I offer a suggestion?"

The professor nodded.

"Many of the *Ostarbeiter* coming to the hospital aren't very proficient in German and we are in dire need of translators. I have found some prisoners here who are fluent in Polish, Russian and German." It was a stretch, but it might just work.

Professor Scherer raised an eyebrow.

"So, if Kommandant Greiner permits, we could take one or two of the prisoners on a work party with us?"

Both men furrowed their brows, seemingly not convinced with the idea.

"A Polish officer would surely help our cause, Herr Professor?"

After some discussion back and forth, it was finally agreed that Anna should choose one prisoner and deliver him to Berlin, where Professor Scherer would personally discuss the expected tasks with him upon his return.

Anna's body hummed with joy, ignoring the need to prevent a meeting between Peter and the professor. That problem she could tackle later.

That same moment, a knock on the door sounded and an emaciated figure entered the room, his eyes trained on the floor. "Please forgive my intrusion, Kommandant Greiner, but may I ask for the nurse's help in a medical emergency?"

Worried the emergency could be Peter or Stan, Anna answered before one of the men had the opportunity to deny the request, "Of course. I'll come with you." She turned to the professor with an apologetic smile. "I'll be right back."

"You have a transfusion syringe?" the prisoner asked her.

She'd seen one in the big medical suitcase and nodded even as she hurried beside the man, "Are you the doctor?"

"Doctor and prisoner," he growled without slowing down his pace.

Her breath stalled when she entered the hospital barracks and saw Peter standing there with a big frown on his forehead, the sleeve of his left arm rolled up. Next, her glance fell on the pallid figure lying on the bunk.

"What's happened?" she hissed, opening her medical bag and retrieving the syringe. Peter's eyes went wide and she noticed a barely visible shiver running down his spine. "Nothing to worry about," she soothed him, although there was a lot to worry about. With his debilitated physical condition and the catastrophic hygienic conditions, the procedure was a huge risk.

"He's fallen and his leg wound opened again," the doctor interjected, taking the equipment from her hands and pointing at Peter to kneel beside the bunk.

"It was my fault," Peter said in a whisper for her ears only.

She shook her head and then watched with horror how the doctor pushed he needle into Peter's arm. "Wait. You have to disinfect the device first."

He didn't even turn around to look at her and continued to do the same with Stan while he mumbled, "Fräulein, you seem to have forgotten where you are." He fastened the hoses and applied the suction to start the blood flow from Peter to Stan, before he addressed Anna again. "If he faints, stop the blood flow immediately. I'll see if I can find a piece of bread for him."

Anna gazed at Peter who, for lack of a chair, knelt on the floor beside his brother, leaning against the bunk. She balled her hands into fists. No patient should be treated in conditions like this.

"I got the permission to take you back to Berlin," she whispered.

"How?" His voice sounded as feeble as he looked. He'd been a strong man less than half a year ago, but fighting in the uprising and captivity had turned him into a shadow of his former self. Her heart bled looking at his sunken cheeks and hollow eyes.

War was beyond cruel.

"I said we could need a translator at the hospital." She didn't mention the tiny problem that Professor Scherer personally wanted to talk to him in his quest to secure goodwill.

Peter shook his head. "It won't work."

"Yes it will. I have a plan. Or you'll die in here." It wasn't unheard of that prisoners escaped during a transport.

"I cannot leave," Peter said after looking at his brother. "He'll die without me. I cannot let this happen."

A wave of fear swallowed her. Breathing became difficult and she saw red dots dancing in front of her eyes. The fear streamed down into her stomach and then surged up her spine again, turning into rage. "Don't be stupid. I'll take you home."

"My home is my family. And while I love you more than anyone else in this world, Stan needs me now. I cannot leave him alone."

She saw how much pride it cost him to say these words, to reject the offer for freedom, the promise for survival. His lips thinned, and he gave her an apologetic gaze full of regret, sorrow, and love. A single tear rolled down her cheek, because she could see the determination in his eyes. She knew there was nothing she could do to convince him to come with her.

"Anna, darling. I'm as heartbroken as you are, but I must do this for Stan. He's my little brother, I cannot leave him alone. You'd do the same."

She nodded. Deep in her heart she understood. She had sacrificed herself for her younger sister, too and she would do it again if she had to. But that didn't make it less tragic.

Pressing a kiss on his lips, she whispered, "I love you. And I'll think of you every day until you return to my side."

CHAPTER 15: ANNA

A nna jumped at the sound of steps and quickly stood up, smoothing her hands down her skirt.

"Both of your patients seem to be fine," she said to the doctor who approached them holding up a tiny piece of awful-smelling bread.

"That's good."

"I should leave," she said more to herself than anyone else and fled from the barracks.

Her feet barely obeyed her, wanting to return to Peter and drag him behind her to safety. Despite her inner turmoil, she managed to mask her expression and assume a businesslike demeanor.

On the short walk to the commandant's office, she passed several British prisoners and the faded uniforms reminded her of Tom, the RAF pilot her sister Ursula had smuggled out of the country. If Peter was too stubborn to let her save him, she could at least save his brother. And she already knew how.

When she entered, the professor and the commandant were deep in discussion and barely raised their heads to acknowledge her. She patiently waited until they finished talking, spinning the story she'd tell them. The professor loved a good challenge and she'd give him one.

"Fräulein Klausen, did you get the emergency sorted out?" the professor asked her.

"Yes, for now, but the man is badly injured. He received a gunshot wound to his leg and shows all the signs of fighting gangrene."

"Gangrene?" The professor's brows shot up. He'd been researching means to medicate this deadly disease and he'd been close to a scientific breakthrough when all research had been relocated from the Charité to the camp in Auschwitz. Anna knew it still rankled him that a mediocre doctor and scientist like Dr. Mengele now reaped all the recognition for his research.

"Yes, Professor. And I believe that this prisoner has the exact specifics needed to be of great scientific benefit to the outstanding work you've done. If we transferred him to a hospital in Berlin, we could study his recovery very closely and hopefully reach the breakthrough you're looking for to find a vaccine."

"We're not officially pursuing research at the moment, as our main priority is to treat patients..." Professor Scherer pushed his glasses up his nose. She could see his excitement mount.

"Which is a well-thought decision of the Führer," Kommandant Greiner said. "There'll be enough time for research after the war."

Anna wanted to yell with frustration, but forced herself

to stay calm and neutral. "We appreciate that the Führer always has the best interests of his people in mind and I would be the last person to question his omniscience." She'd have to lay it on thick to get to her goal. What she was about to say would probably see her hanged if the truth were ever discovered, but since she was already in deep, she might as well forge ahead.

She combined a shy smile with batting her eyes. From underneath her long eyelashes, she schmoozed, "I was reluctant to tell you, because I'm not absolutely certain, but this prisoner looked so familiar." She took a deep breath. "I took the opportunity to question him to see if I was correct. He was barely conscious and I believe he only gave away his true identity, because of his weak condition."

"Identity?" the commandant inquired, his attention now fully focused directly on her.

"Yes, sir. Your prisoner is in fact the first cousin of Stanisław Mikołajczyk, the Prime Minister of the Polish government in exile."

The commandant gave her an incredulous look and then turned to the professor. "What is she talking about?"

"Fräulein Klausen, you cannot honestly believe this?" Professor Scherer gave her an indulgent look.

"Even if he is who he says he is, the Polish government in exile is a bunch of criminals acting up against the German Reich. The prisoner should be executed right away for the revolt his cousin schemed in Warsaw. It has cost us tens of thousands of valiant soldiers," the commandant said, a bulging vein throbbing on his temple.

The room seemed to shrink in size and Anna felt a heavy weight pressing her down. This was not going the way she'd planned it. The mere possibility of Stan's being executed because of her lie made her heart gallop.

Anna played up her expression and then lowered her voice as if they were all involved in keeping a secret. "I agree. And I told him such, but the bold man simply smiled and threatened me that Winston Churchill personally would see justice done, since he's Churchill's godson." At the mention of the British Prime Minister's name, both of the men gave her a dubious look.

"I still don't believe the prisoner is telling the truth," the commandant murmured.

"But what if he is? There would be no harm in saving this one prisoner. Should worst come to worst, his godfather will know whom to thank for his survival."

The commandant nodded thoughtfully and Anna stayed silent, letting the two men work things out between them. She'd tempted them with plump, juicy bait. Bait so good they had to agree. At least that's what she hoped for.

Prayed for.

Professor Scherer surely wouldn't pass up an opportunity to endear himself to Churchill personally. A boon he could exploit once the war was over. If the commandant were only half-clever he'd see the same opportunity.

After an endless wait, the commandant straightened his shoulders and looked at her. "Very well, you may take this man back to Berlin with you. I'll sign the papers."

A weight fell from Anna's shoulders and her legs itched to dance around the offices with unadulterated joy.

"That is immensely clear-sighted of you, Kommandant," the professor said and added, "In this case, we won't take the other prisoner for translation work, because we don't want to cause undue investigation."

Showers of cold water soaked Anna's heart when she heard the comment, but she consoled herself with the knowledge that she could at least get Stan out of here.

Under normal conditions any doctor worth his salt wouldn't allow Stan to be transported anywhere, especially not in the back of a vehicle. But not even Anna dared to ask for an ambulance to transport a prisoner of war. If Stan had only half the determination of his older brother, he'd clutch on to his life like a dog to a bone.

"We need to hurry, Professor, since my wife doesn't like to wait with dinner," the commandant said. "Fräulein Klausen, I will arrange the papers first thing in the morning. Please enjoy the hospitality in our guest house for the night. My secretary will arrange accommodation and food for you."

"Thank you, sir."

Anna sighed. She hated to stay here. Now she had to worry the next twelve hours that something might go wrong.

CHAPTER 16: STAN

Impenetrable fog clouded his vision. Voices reached his ears but he couldn't make out the words. Straining his ears, he recognized his brother's voice and a woman. The nurse.

Piotr's wife.

She'd come to take his brother to Berlin. He wanted to scream, tell them to stay. But at the same time he knew it was selfish. His leg wasn't getting any better and at the rate his condition was worsening he'd be dead before Christmas.

He wasn't afraid. The past five years with the partisans in Poland had taught him to cope with the fear. It came, washed over him and settled deep down in his stomach, reminding him to be alert. Keeping him on his toes and never letting him feel invincible. The fear had often been his lifesaver, and had prevented him from becoming reckless.

Now he was past fear. There was nothing he could do. Death wasn't something he was afraid of, not anymore.

Jarek waited for him on the other side, his parents, and so many of his friends.

Piotr and...Anna. They were talking about him. She was crying. He could hear the sadness in her voice. What had happened?

The fog thinned out. Two shapes at his bed. Two men. Where had the nurse gone?

"Stan? Are you alright?" Peter asked with barely concealed worry in his tone.

Alright? Here? Now? He couldn't form words. He couldn't even move his head to nod. So he batted his eyelids to signal that he'd heard.

"Thank God. I'm so sorry. It was my fault, I shouldn't have..."

Where was Anna? And why was Piotr still here? Who was the other person?

"Your brother saved your life with a blood transfusion," the Polish doctor said.

A *blood transfusion?* In a *prison camp?* He must be hallucinating. This wasn't possible.

"You can stay here until the morning," the doctor said. "Keep him warm. If he's still alive in the morning, he might just survive."

"Stan. I'm sorry. I won't ever leave your side. I'll stay here and take care of you," Peter said.

Stan slowly moved his head, blinking several times to clear the haze. It was only the two of them. The doctor had left. He cleared his throat, but still no sound came out. Peter put a cup of water to his lips. After a few sips he cleared his throat again.

"Why are you still here?" he whispered.

"I'm not leaving you."

"That's stupid. Go after her and tell her you changed your mind. You won't be able to save me, but you can at least save yourself."

"That's where you are wrong." Peter cast him a grim stare. "We're both going to survive this bloody war."

Stan made an attempt to protest his brother's stupidity but he was too weak to even shake his head. Seeing the stubborn glint in Peter's eyes he knew there was nothing he could say to change his mind anyway.

"Thanks, man." He closed his eyes, determined to prove his brother right and survive.

When he woke up in the morning, Peter lay crouched by his side and a warm feeling spread through his body. *I'm a lucky bastard.* Just looking at his brother gave him a sliver of hope.

Moments later, Bartosz sneaked into the hospital barracks. "Hey, here you are. The nurse is back. I heard rumors she's taking some famous prisoner to Berlin. A cousin of Stanisław Mikołajczyk."

"Our prime minister? You sure? If one of the lads were his cousin, we'd know." Peter rubbed his beard.

"Yes, that's what's kinda strange. But they seem convinced he's someone super-important and will take him to Berlin with them."

Stan looked from one man to the other. This kind of action was highly unusual. At least he'd never heard about such things happening. But if this Polish prisoner really belonged to the upper crust, the Nazis might want to keep him separate from the rest.

They grew silent, each one alone with his thoughts,

when the door flew open and Anna entered the room with a man in SS uniform in tow. Stan could barely hold back a gasp, glancing at Peter and Bartosz, who seemed as surprised as he was.

"What does she want here?" Peter whispered.

"No idea. But we need to leave for roll call," Bartosz answered.

"Go. I'm not going anywhere." Stan waved them both off, trying to make it sound like a joke for their benefit, but inside, he was sure that his time was running out fast.

CHAPTER 17: PETER

Peter walked towards Anna, pondering whether it would be prudent to talk to her or not. Bartosz didn't know, and the SS man at her side looked the part. His glance fell on the man's shining belt buckle with the inscription *Gott mit uns*, In God we trust. He pursed his lips; surely God wasn't very happy about the horrific crimes committed in his name.

Anna gave him a look that meant for him to keep his mouth shut and then said, "We've come here to retrieve the prisoner Zdanek."

Peter's eyes almost popped out of his head and he had to bite his lips to remain silent.

She waved at Bartosz. "You, go with Professor Scherer's driver and find something we can use as a stretcher. And you," she pointed at Peter, "come with me to make the prisoner ready for transport."

"Do you think this is a good idea?" the SS man said.

Anna only smiled at him. "Do you really think this man

will dare to do me any harm, Hans? In any case I can yell if I need your help."

Hans smirked. "I'll gladly shoot him through the skull should he so much as hurt a hair on your head."

That was an unconcealed threat towards Peter, who played his part in the little game and put on a frightened expression. "I assure you, I won't make any problems. I want to live."

Hans showed a gratified smile and Peter wondered why Professor Scherer put up with this miserable, spineless SS brute. Or hadn't he had a choice as to who became his new driver? Bartosz left with Hans and Peter followed Anna to Stan's bed.

"How? Why? Is he the Prime Minister's cousin?" he whispered.

"And Churchill's godson. I had to think of something. Since you are too stubborn to come with me, I can at least rescue your brother." Her hand snaked into his. The skin so soft. Cool and warm at the same time. Tiny. She was so small compared to him, and yet she had the inner strength of ten men. And the stubbornness of a mule.

"I love you," he whispered, yearning to kiss her. But with the SS brute due to return any minute, he didn't dare.

They reached the bunk where Stan lay and she bent down to give him instructions. "I'm here to take you to Berlin to a proper hospital. A place where you will receive state-of-the-art treatment for your leg and the infection."

Peter watched the disbelieving gaze in his brother's eyes and hurried to add in Polish that he had to pretend to be Mikołajczyk's cousin. Stan's eyes widened even more while Anna removed his blanket and hid a gasp at the putrid smell coming from beneath. All three of them knew that going with her was Stan's only chance to survive. They heard heavy footfalls approaching the barracks and she reached into her pockets.

"Take this. It's all I could organize last night." She slid several packages of cigarettes and half a loaf of bread into Peter's pockets and squeezed his hand for a moment. "I would rather take you both out of here."

"Me, too, but knowing that Stan is in good care will keep me strong. Don't worry about me," Peter said, his voice at the point of breaking. He might put on a brave face, but his own chances of survival were slim in this hovel.

The door slammed open and Bartosz returned with the SS man. "There's nothing to use as a stretcher," Hans said.

"Then we'll carry him to the automobile," Anna answered.

"You're not expecting me to carry that stinking piece of trash?" Hans gave Stan a nasty stare and Peter fisted his hands to keep himself from strangling the Nazi bastard.

Thankfully, Anna never lost her composure and said with a wave of her hand, "Off course not, you would only dirty your impeccable uniform. He will do it." She pointed at Peter. "Why don't you go ahead and put a tarpaulin on the backseat of the limousine? Professor Scherer wouldn't be happy if it got dirty."

Hans nodded, seemingly relieved to be allowed to leave the hospital barracks with the annoyance of the moaning and groaning men.

Bartosz gave an apologetic glance to Peter murmuring, "I'd better go to roll call," before he disappeared, too.

Peter could understand him. The hospital barracks

wasn't a place where anyone wanted to spend more time than absolutely necessary, and being late for roll call would draw undue and unwelcome attention to him.

With everyone gone, Peter grabbed Anna and pressed a feverish kiss on her lips. She was thinner than he remembered, but still soft and warm. Her curves pressed against his body and stirred a reaction. He gave a loud sigh, wondering whether he'd made the right decision. He might not hold her in his arms ever again. But one glance at the pale, sweaty face of his brother encouraged him.

I'm doing the right thing. For Stan.

"I love you so much," Anna whispered against his mouth.

Her tender words tore his heart apart. "I love you just as much."

Anna pulled away from him, her cheeks flushed and her lips swollen from the rough kiss. "We have to go."

She averted her eyes, but he took her chin and moved it upward. "Don't be sad, darling. Remember, bad weeds grow tall. I have experienced worse. I'll be just fine."

He could see she didn't believe one word he said, but did her best to put on a brave face. Peter clenched his hands into fists in his pockets as despair filled him. Both of them knew this could well be the last time they saw one another. She would have no reason to visit this particular camp again. There would be no second rescue plan for Peter.

Stan gave an awful scream when they moved him onto Peter's back, and Peter almost succumbed to the weight of his brother. Four months ago he wouldn't have flinched carrying double the weight, but malnourishment and catastrophic conditions had made a wreck out of him.

For a moment he doubted whether he could withstand

whatever fate held in store until the Allies would – finally – liberate them. Nobody he knew doubted the impending victory of the Allies. It was simply a question of when and not a question of if. But many men doubted whether they'd still be around by the time the Nazis were finally defeated.

The walk to the professor's limousine with the heavy cargo on his shoulders seemed endless and Peter stumbled more than once, sheer willpower holding him upright. He dropped Stan onto the tarpaulin in the back of the Mercedes, sending Anna a pleading gaze.

She understood and engaged the SS man in a conversation, taking them several steps away from the automobile and giving the two brothers a few minutes to say their goodbyes.

Stan tried to remain stoic, but Peter wasn't fooled. He could see the evocative emotions in his brother's eyes.

"You'll be fine. Anna will take good care of you," he said with the most nonchalant tone he could muster.

"I'll never forget what you did for me." Stan fought back tears, holding on to his composure only by a thin thread. "I won't disappoint you. And once I'm back on my feet, I'll watch out for your wife."

Peter squeezed Stan's hand. "Give my son a kiss for me, will you?"

"I will. Take care of yourself."

Heavy footfalls approached the vehicle and Peter quickly moved a blanket over Stan and backed out. He almost smacked into the SS man Hans and excused himself. With a last longing gaze towards Anna, he returned to his barracks and to an unknown fate.

CHAPTER 18: STAN

Berlin, the Charité clinic

The ride to Berlin passed in a blur. Fever wracked Stan's body and each bump in the road – and there were many – ripped a fresh wave of pain through his body. He kept his eyes closed, breathing through the pain and biting his lips so as not to scream.

Despite his effort to focus on breathing, he still overheard the conversation between Anna and the SS man who acted as driver. If he'd had the strength, Stan would have punched the despicable man for his disgraceful remarks about Jews, Slavs and prisoners in general.

Back in Poland with the partisans this Hans person wouldn't have lasted another second, but now Stan contented himself with plans of revenge and deciding on the slowest and most torturous method of death for the SS man. At least it kept him busy and distracted from the pain ravaging his body.

Anna glanced at him several times and once insisted Hans stop so she could rearrange Stan on the backseat after a particularly nasty road hole had catapulted him into the small space between the back seat and the back of the driver's seat.

"Are you alright?" she asked him with an angelical smile.

After helping him up, she pressed a cup of cool water to his lips and wiped cold sweat from his forehead. Right in that moment, when he saw the genuine concern in her beautiful blue eyes, he understood why Peter had fallen in love with her. This woman was truly special, with a kind heart and a will of steel.

"More or less. But I will be when this ride is over." He tried a grin, but saw from the worry etched into her face that she'd seen right through his façade. Had seen the awful throes racking his body. Had noticed the gritted teeth and labored breathing.

And the experienced nurse also knew that his body was about to fail him.

"Sleep if you can," she said and returned to the passenger seat.

Stan couldn't understand how she could put up with the sleazy driver who not only constantly uttered hateful diatribes, but also tried to hit on her. Thankfully, dizziness engulfed him and he fell into oblivion.

He woke, his entire body burning with a fire so hot he thought he'd landed straight in hell. People tore at his limbs and moved him around, intensifying the agony tenfold.

"I'm sorry, we need to disinfect the wounds," a soft voice said, but he'd long stopped caring and screamed at the top of his lungs.

Then he fell back into the welcome blackness of unconsciousness.

~

"This is the prisoner, he's been unconscious for most of the last days," Anna said.

Stan felt the soft mattress beneath him and tried to remember what had happened. Oh yes, the ride to the hospital. Pain. More pain than he'd ever experienced before. Screaming. Cool comforting blackness.

He blinked and slowly opened his eyes, distinguishing several shadows bent over his bed.

"You're awake. That's good," a deep, pleasant voice said and a man in his fifties with salt and pepper hair, wearing glasses and a white lab coat, rounded the bed. "You're at the Charité clinic. My name is Professor Scherer and I will personally see that you receive the best possible care in order to heal."

"Thank you," Stan said with a hoarse voice, suppressing the smirk he wanted to show.

If Anna hadn't lied and told them he was the godson of the British prime minister this professor wouldn't give a shit whether he died or not. He just hoped, for Anna's and his own benefit, that nobody ever found out the truth.

"Let's see the progress," the professor said and a young nurse stepped forward.

She pushed his clean-smelling nightgown aside and busied herself removing the bandages on his thigh. Despite her gentleness it hurt and he flinched for a moment.

"I'm sorry," she said, leaving Stan wondering the last time someone had apologized for treating him roughly.

"No big deal," he managed to croak out.

Despite his weak condition he appreciated the proper figure of the nurse and his mind drifted off into a land of precious fantasies. With his thigh exposed he managed a glimpse at the green pus oozing from his injury. Most of his fiery red thigh itched.

Another doctor stepped forward, examining the wound, every touch making Stan grit his teeth harder. When the poking finally stopped, the doctors talked in low voices while the peachy nurse set out to make a new bandage. He couldn't understand most of their words, but the grave expressions on their faces conveyed a clear message.

Stan was not healing well.

As soon as the nurse finished tending to him, she informed the doctors.

Professor Scherer returned to his side, saying, "The bullet was removed in the camp already, but I'm afraid an infection has settled into the flesh."

Even Stan knew that the operation in the prisoner camp had been done under awful hygienic conditions, and an infection was almost to be expected. He trusted his bear-like constitution and believed it would all heal well. Although when he looked down his body, instead of strong muscles he saw only bones protruding from flaps of skin.

Another person entered the room, but Stan didn't have the energy to turn his head and look at them.

"Ah, Nurse Anna, you are here," one of the doctors said.

Anna approached his bed, giving him a warning gaze.

She'd made it perfectly clear to him during the trip that nobody was to know they knew each other.

"He looks a lot better," she said. Even though she avoided his eyes, he could clearly hear the fakeness in her tone. He did not look better. He was not healing well.

"The progress is slower than desirable," Professor Scherer said and leaned down to Stan, peering into his eyes. "You look vaguely familiar."

Stan had no idea what to answer and preferred to keep quiet. Thankfully the professor didn't pursue the topic and instead commented, "His eyes are still feverish."

Anna dutifully noted the remark and asked, "Should I give him something to lower the fever?"

"Not yet, but make sure he drinks enough." The professor stood and gazed at Stan again, their eyes meeting for a moment, before he turned to Anna. "Don't you think he bears a remarkable resemblance to Peter Wolf?"

Stan watched how Anna nearly choked and then he did the same when his brain processed that Peter Wolf was the fake identity of his brother. Thankfully Anna was more quick-witted than he was and cocked her head as if thinking before she answered with a smile, "Not really. The only thing remotely similar are the blue eyes."

"You're right. It must be the eyes."

Ever so slowly, Stan hissed out the breath he'd been holding and sent a prayer to the heavens that the professor wouldn't pursue the topic.

CHAPTER 19: PETER

Hunger pangs attacked him and he lit one of the precious cigarettes to make it go away. For the umpteenth time he cursed himself for turning a deaf ear to Anna's pleas to help him escape. He could be somewhere less awful than this place, with food to fill his stomach and winter clothing to keep him warm.

An hour later it was finally dinnertime and he presented his empty bowl to the man in charge of distributing the soup, watching like a hawk that the ladle was filled to the brim. One, two...the man stopped.

"Hey, the ration is three ladles of soup," Peter protested.

"Sorry, chap. Not today. They cut the provisions again," the man answered stoically and waved him away. The other prisoners in line pushed at his back, eager to get whatever little food they could.

The constant hunger was the worst. The cold, the boredom, the rough treatment, even the hard work – nothing compared to the gnawing at the intestines the hunger caused. Peter took his bowl and a tiny piece of bread and returned to his barracks, sitting next to Bartosz.

"My mother makes the most delicious *piroggi*," Bartosz said with a dreamy expression on his face.

Peter spooned his soup, the image of small filled dumplings forming in his mind, while Bartosz continued, "Her piroggi dough is the finest in all of our district. She grinds the flour herself and adds a generous drop of fresh butter from our cows to it…"

All eyes flew to Bartosz, everyone eager to hear about yet another delightful treat from the past. "…then she would take minced meat, from cattle not from pigs, and add an onion, salt and pepper to it…" Peter's mouth watered as he listened intently to Bartosz's descriptions and he deluded himself into tasting delicious piroggi instead of the awful dishwater-like soup he was eating. "…then she would add whatever vegetables she had, mostly mushrooms, or tomatoes chopped into tiny pieces…"

By now the experience of eating piroggi completely overwhelmed Peter and his spirit had escaped to a better time when his own mother had still been alive and made this popular Polish dish for her four children. He took up the description where Bartosz left off and added, "We children would beg our mother to roast the piroggi in the pan after boiling them. She'd use a generous amount of butter and the scrumptious smell of roasted piroggi would soon fill the house."

Everyone in the barracks sighed, as imaginary smells wafted through the air. "She then served the golden piroggi with a light brown crust and each child could eat as many as we wanted." Wistful sighs roamed the barracks. "Biting into these delicacies was almost like going straight to heaven." Peter took another spoonful of disgusting soup and sniffed it, eager to recognize the smell of roasted piroggi.

Another prisoner added, "My wife always served them with warm milk fresh from our cows. When I came home after a hard day of work in the fields, she was always waiting for me with fatty, creamy warm milk with every meal."

Peter licked out his bowl as to not let a single drop of liquid go to waste. Talking about bygone feasts and delicacies was one way to entertain each other and outfox the gnawing hunger – at least for a few minutes. All too soon reality would rear its ugly head again and attack everyone with hunger pangs so strong that the men buckled under the impact.

Shortly before Christmas restlessness seized the camp. Rumors spread. Gossip mushroomed. Accurate information stayed elusive because the German guards only related the official information of German victories. But new prisoners brought the news that the Allied forces had reached the Rhine.

Peter smiled at this piece of information. Now it wouldn't be long until the Allies crushed the depleted Wehrmacht and liberated the prisoners of war. Hopes soared in the camp and most everyone wore a wistful smile on their face. They might even be free before the New Year.

Peter already made mental plans to go to Berlin and find his family. A few days later his hopes were crushed as the guards told the prisoners about an offensive in the Ardennes called *Unternehmen Wacht am Rhein*, Operation Watch on the Rhine, initiated by the Wehrmacht to recapture the harbor of Antwerp and prevent the Allies from landing fresh supplies.

On the morning of 16 December 1944, the Germans completely surprised the Allies by attacking a weakly defended section of the front line. Since the Allies' superior air forces were grounded by the heavily overcast weather conditions, the Wehrmacht scored some quick successes.

Bartosz frowned and whispered, "Do you believe this?"

"I guess at least part of it is true. They haven't been telling us blatant lies, although they sure know which parts to include and which to leave out," Peter answered, wondering how much territory the Wehrmacht had actually recaptured.

The guards enjoyed rubbing salt into the wounds of the prisoners and relayed every last detail of the successful attack. "Watch out, losers. Now we're going to crush you. Our Wehrmacht will encircle and destroy your armies and before the year is over, you'll beg to negotiate a peace treaty. Once this is wrapped up, our Führer can fully concentrate on the Eastern Front and smash the Ivan."

The morale in the camp plummeted. Although nobody believed the Germans would be successful with this lunatic endeavor, it certainly meant a considerable delay in the upcoming liberation. More than one of the men wondered how much longer he'd be around. And if he'd ever bear witness to the downfall of the Third Reich.

A few days later members of the International Red Cross arrived to distribute parcels from the family members of the inmates. Just in time for Christmas, the mood surged with the food found inside.

Bartosz carried a package from his mother, and after seeing Peter sitting empty-handed, sat down besides him. "We'll share. And the next time we're allowed to write a postcard, you send it to your sister."

"Thanks." Peter gave his new friend a warm smile.

His sister Katrina and her boyfriend lived Bartosz's farm in Poland with Bartosz's mother, but so far he hadn't been able to let her know he was alive.

The package was filled to the brim with goods from the farm. Cheese, hard cured sausages, flour, a jar of jam, and dried vegetables. The good woman had even squeezed long underwear and socks into the small box. On the bottom was a postcard, some of the words censored with black ink.

Bartosz pressed the Red Cross issued card against his heart and his face took on a dreamy expression. "One day I'll see her again. I just hope we both make it through the war."

"It won't be long now. The guards can say all they want about the Ardennes offensive, but I doubt the winning streak of the Germans can last. With the Americans fully involved our side has so much more manpower and material…we'll win sooner or later."

"Sooner, I hope," Bartosz answered absentmindedly as he started to read the postcard. "My mom's fine, but she won't be able to send another package once the Soviets reach our land."

"Your mother is a kind-hearted person. The Soviets are about to conquer her village and all she worries about is sending a package to you?" Peter said, knowing full well that the so-called liberators ran rampant in Poland, stealing, killing and raping, not differentiating between German, Polish or even Jewish women freshly escaped from the horrors of the camps.

"She is worried about the Soviets, but she'll manage. They, too, need the food of the farmers. She writes that she's glad for the help of Katrina and Richard. With all of us boys gone..."

Peter put a hand on Bartosz's shoulder, whose three brothers had all been killed in action. He didn't try to console him with words, because what was there to say?

Nothing. Life was hard and war was unjust.

CHAPTER 20: ANNA

Christmas 1944

Christmas Eve had arrived but it was a somber affair. Despite the uplifting rallying cries coming from the *Goebbels Schnauze*, as they called the small radio, nobody in their right mind still believed in a German victory. Anna secretly hoped for a quick end to the war.

Mutter always favored the old German proverb: *Lieber ein Ende mit Schrecken als ein Schrecken ohne Ende*. Better a terrible end than unending terror. Anna sighed, because she'd never voice it publicly. But despite the police state, people still expressed their mindsets in the subtlest of ways.

If only those god-awful nightly air raids would stop. Didn't the English and Americans get bored with dropping their bombs and shells on a city that already lay in ruins? Every morning Anna had to climb across fresh heaps of rubble on her way to work.

Ursula had insisted they attend church. Because of the

curfew, the Holy Mass was held in the afternoon instead of the traditional hour of midnight.

"Are you ready?" Ursula called out to her.

"Almost." Anna draped a knitted shawl around her shoulders, her thoughts with Peter, who didn't have the luxury of warm winter clothing. With a last glance at the mirror she put on her hat and a pair of gloves.

Jan rushed into the hallway, sliding across the polished linoleum, and skidded to a halt right in front of her. "Can we build a snowman on the way?"

"No, we cannot. We're already late. But we can on the way back." She smiled at the young boy who'd whirled into her life and her heart two months ago. She observed him a few moments and shook her head. "Your trousers are too short again. And your shoes!"

"It's not my fault, because my toes are too big for them." Jan wiggled his big toe through the hole in his shoes. Buying new shoes was as impossible as buying real coffee nowadays.

"I'll ask at church if someone has a half-decent pair in your size." She sighed.

"Let me see tomorrow if I can cut down one of Richard's pairs of trousers for you," Mutter said. Anna shared a look with her sister Ursula.

Their mother had defended the few remaining things of their brother Richard with teeth and claws, saving them for when he returned. Her willingness to mend them for Jan showed just how much she loved her step-grandson.

"I'm sure Richard's fine," Anna said.

Last time they heard from him he'd requested a transfer to the Eastern front. She knew Mutter still resented his decision, but Anna suspected that he'd had reasons for such a drastic measure. Since then they hadn't heard from him. She stuck to the thinking that no news was good news.

Ursula put on her coat, gloves and hat and then went to retrieve Eveline. The six-month-old baby made gurgling sounds and scrunched her cute face into a smile. Anna smiled back, tickling the baby's tummy with her fingers. Little Evie was the one thing sure to bring a smile to Anna's face, no matter how bad her day at work had been or how morose her thoughts.

"Here, hold her for a minute." Ursula handed the baby to Anna, while she fetched a blanket to swaddle her.

Finally, they walked down the stairs into a sunny but cold winter day. Anna remembered winters years ago when the freshly fallen white snow would transform into a greyish muddy mass beneath the wheels of the automobiles. Since a motorized vehicle rarely passed this place anymore, the snow still covered the asphalt, mercifully hiding rubble, potholes and other signs of destruction beneath a glimmering blanket.

If only all the hardships of war could be swept under the carpet as easily. Anna gave a loud sigh and Jan squeezed his small hand into hers.

"I'm sure he's fine," said Ursula, who had guessed her sister's thoughts.

"I'm sure he is," Anna repeated, although her heart broke at the memory of Peter's rawboned figure in the patched-up uniform. Tears threatened to spill as she tried to imagine the Christmas celebration – or lack thereof – he would have.

After the mass they returned home to prepare their meager Christmas feast.

"You go and play with Jan outside," Mutter said as they reached the front door of their building, which miraculously stood tall and erect despite the devastation surrounding it.

"We'll be back in half an hour," Anna answered with a smile to show she'd understood. Jan was too old to believe in the *Christkind,* the little angel Christ Child anymore, but they'd give her mother the satisfaction of setting out the presents and pretending someone else had done it.

She wrapped the shawl tighter around her shoulders and took off to engage in a snowball fight with Jan. Minutes later she was puffing and blowing, heat from the exercise making the shawl unnecessary.

A cold mass hit her square in the neck and she turned to see Jan raising his fist into the air. "Got you!"

She giggled, all the worries and sorrow falling away for a few minutes of blissful childish play. When she heard the tolling of the bells, she glanced at her wristwatch. Half an hour had passed and then some. "Let's go upstairs. We'd better not keep your grandma waiting."

Jan nodded with a serious face, asking, "Does she really think I still believe in the *Christkind?*"

"Probably not. But we shouldn't deny her the pleasure. What do you think?" She wrapped her arm around Jan's shoulders and he leaned into her.

"I wish my dad was here."

"Me too." To spare the poor boy the disappointment, she hadn't told him about her failed attempt to rescue Peter from the camp. "But I may have a surprise for you."

"What is it?" His eyes lit up with joy and curiosity.

"A surprise. So I can't tell you, but it's something really good." She grinned, enjoying the anticipation on his face. She hadn't told him about Stan either, because the boy's uncle had been in such a delicate condition. Now he seemed to be over the worst and would surely appreciate a visit from his nephew.

CHAPTER 21: STAN

L ying in his bed, Stan cursed himself and the world. He'd been at the Charité for weeks, but his progress was much slower than anticipated. Anna visited him every day to keep him company for a few minutes, but he still felt lonely and had too much time to think.

Every time he thought about Piotr and their last minutes, a deep sadness consumed him and he struggled with guilt. It was his fault Piotr remained behind at the camp. His brother had sacrificed his own freedom to give him a chance to heal. And what did he do to repay his generosity? Not heal! At least not fast enough.

That damn leg was still rife with infection. He wasn't dumb. Despite the fact that nobody told him the truth about his condition, he could see the concern etched into the faces of the doctors and nurse. Anna rarely looked him in the eyes and when she told him he'd made great progress and would soon be alright, he knew she lied.

Stan scoffed into the room. Piotr's sacrifice would be in

vain if he died. *I'm not going to die!* That's what he told himself day after day, hour after hour, but how on earth could he command his stubborn leg to heal?

As Christmas approached, Stan fell into a deep depression, thoughts of being useless consuming him. Piotr should have been saved, not him. He was one of the worthless non-walking wounded. Piotr should be enjoying his freedom and his wife. Piotr should have left him to die in Fallingbostel. If anything happened to Piotr, how could he live with his guilt?

And today, with everyone flitting around and flaunting their Christmas spirit, his day turned several shades darker.

"Christmas! I dare you, God. Why don't you work a miracle? Prove it, because I'm starting to believe you can't!" Stan's anger snaked up his spine as he yelled the words into the room. The other patients were either too weak to acknowledge his outburst or just raised an eye at the alien language.

The next moment, guilt about his blasphemy attacked him, knocking the air from his lungs. He half expected an angry God to appear and send him straight into purgatory.

But instead the door opened to a lanky boy.

Who the hell...?

The boy stormed into the room, stopping for a moment to scan the patients. Then he rushed towards Stan and wrapped his scrawny arms around Stan's shoulders.

"Uncle Stan. I'm so happy." Stan's brain was still working slowly and he didn't understand most of the monologue the boy whispered into his ear. But when wetness soaked the skin of his neck, Stan finally grasped the truth. The boy was Janusz. Piotr's son.

He remembered Anna telling him, but he hadn't really paid attention to her actual words.

"It's really you? How? Why?"

Jan crawled up on the bed with Stan and hugged him close. "Anna brought me here. She thought you might like company. Today is Christmas, you know?"

"I know. It's my leg that's injured, not my brains," Stan chuckled, the boy's presence returning some of his will to live.

"I brought you a present. Here." Jan produced several biscuits from his pocket. "We all saved up our sugar rations and Grandma made them."

Grandma? Stan took a biscuit and savored the sweet taste. As the flavor exploded across his tongue, he moaned. He hadn't had a treat in so long. Whoever this Grandma was, she sure knew how to bake. While Stan munched the sweets, Jan bombarded him with whispered questions.

"Did you see my dad? Is he well? Where is he now? And how did Anna get you out of the camp? Did she rescue you like the German soldier rescued me?"

"Wait..." Stan chuckled. "How am I supposed to answer all these questions when you don't even pause to breathe?"

Jan made a guilty face. "I'm just so excited to see you. Do you think the war will be over soon? And can we all go back home then? Are Katrina and Richard fine? And have you heard about Aunt Agnieska? The last time I saw her was in the transit camp in Warsaw. Do you think they deported her?"

"Slow down." Stan put his free hand on Jan's shoulder, wondering how he could sugarcoat things for the boy. "Your dad is fine, but he misses you terribly. He's thinking about you all the time."

"I miss him too. And my mom." Jan's face fell. "Anna is nice. Her family too, but she's not my mom…"

Tears threatened to spill and Stan quickly thought of a distraction. "Did you get a present for Christmas?"

"Yes." Even in the darkness Stan could see the happiness shining in Jan's face. "Grandma knitted a pullover for me, and Aunt Ursula gave me a real pocket knife. It's so useful. I would show it to you, but Anna didn't allow me to bring it with me."

Stan had difficulties staying serious but nodded and said, "I agree with Anna. A hospital is no place to bring a knife."

They talked for what seemed like hours until their conversation grew sparser and sleep claimed them both. Stan's last thought was that he probably should send Jan home or else Anna would be worried…

The hospital brimmed with activities, the noise of the morning routines waking Stan. Much to his surprise he found Jan still snuggled in his arms, sound asleep. A burst of panic surged through him – the nurses could not find Jan here. Despite being treated like a normal patient, he was still a prisoner, an enemy of the Reich.

"Jan. Jan, wake up. It's morning. You have to leave."

Jan woke, sat up, rubbed his eyes, and then froze when he looked out the window and saw the sun peek over the horizon. "Oh no! I didn't mean to fall asleep here."

Noises outside the room announced the arrival of the morning nurse and Stan pushed Jan off the bed. "Quickly, hide in the closet and don't make a sound."

Jan rushed silently across the floor and had just closed

the closet door behind him when a young nurse entered the room.

Stan lay back on the bed, his heart pumping violently as the tension in his body mounted.

~

Later in the day, Anna visited him and when no other nurse was within earshot asked, "How did you like your Christmas surprise?"

"I'm sorry, if you were worried—"

Anna cut him off. "I figured he was safer in the hospital than wandering the streets alone at night. He's a resourceful boy…" She sighed, giving Stan reason to think it challenging to raise a boy, especially one who wasn't your biological child.

She came to his bedside and pulled a chair over so that she could sit beside him. "We're short on staff so I only have a few minutes, but I thought you might want to see photographs of my family." She held out a small pile and then explained, "This is one of me and my sisters. Lotte, the youngest, she's the one with the fiery curls. And to the left is Ursula, the oldest. She has a baby called Evie." Anna produced a photograph of baby Evie and her grandmother.

Stan took the next picture and pushed himself up higher in the bed. "Who is this?"

"My brother."

The boy in the photograph looked awfully familiar. Younger, but… "What's his name?"

"Richard."

Stan felt waves of dizziness rushing across him as he

sought to grasp the reality laid out before him. "Your… your….brother Richard…is he…? Was he…? I mean was he ever in Poland?"

"In fact, he was stationed in Lodz for a while, but…" She broke off, gazing at Stan. "Why do you ask?"

"I know him. He's the German soldier who rescued Jan. He's my sister Katrina's boyfriend."

Anna's jaw fell to the floor and she stared at him with wide eyes. "Is he…alive?"

"Last time I saw him he and Katrina sought refuge at a friend's farm."

Tears pooled in Anna's eyes and her voice cracked as she took the photograph back, brushing a finger over the image. "That's the best news I have heard in a long time. We were all so worried after his last letter."

Stan had no idea what Richard might have written to his family, but with everything that had happened, they had every reason to be worried. "Your brother has picked up the Polish language quite well; he doesn't have much problem blending in."

"Thank you." Anna touched his arm for a moment, but voices coming from the doorway spurred her to stand up. "I need to go."

CHAPTER 22: PETER

Peter hadn't expected bells and whistles to celebrate Christmas, but seeing all the nostalgic, dreary faces of his fellow prisoners tore at his heart. As children they'd welcomed the freshly fallen snow, a *White Christmas* everyone's dream. Now it was yet another nuisance they had to endure.

Soggy shoes and frozen clothes. Damp underwear and bones that never really warmed up. The men huddled in the barracks heated with their self-made ovens. Whenever those on work parties outside the camp managed to scrounge a few pieces of coal or fallen branches, they dragged them back to use as fuel.

Everyone had saved up food from the parcels the Red Cross had distributed several days ago and now cooked their own festive meals, thanks to one of the Polish mechanics. The fellow had ordered everyone to save up tin cans and with a haphazard-looking device he'd somehow managed to melt the edges together to build a stove that could be heated with wood.

Peter suspiciously eyed the smoke coming from the stove, but the mechanic assured him this was a foolproof thing. Every man pitched in an ingredient and soon they were sitting on their bunks. One man started singing Christmas carols and everyone joined in. It sounded hoarse and squeaky but nonetheless brought back memories of years past when they were free and life was good.

After the sumptuous meal – at least by camp standards – he tucked a hand into his pocket and fingered the cigarettes Anna had given him. *Anna.* She was constantly on his mind, along with Stan and Jan. Thinking of her tore his insides apart, but at the same time, it gave him a strange comfort to know she was somewhere out there.

He retrieved two cigarettes and offered one to Bartosz, who gladly took it and lit it at the open fire in the stove.

"Not that bad. I'm almost full. Certainly more than any other day since my arrival here," Bartosz said.

"Yes, the parcels from home really helped. Thanks for sharing," Peter said with a guilty glance at his friend. Bartosz could have saved the entire food supply for himself and it would have lasted much longer.

"Man, Stan's my best friend. You have no idea how many times he saved my ass these past years."

Peter couldn't answer because one of the older soldiers suggested they act out a Christmas story. At least once a year they could be remotely happy, although he hoped they wouldn't experience another Christmas in captivity. This damned war had to end. After being in the thick of the bloodletting in Warsaw and the news rushing in from the

Ardennes, Peter doubted there'd be many men left to carry on the fighting.

Maybe the Americans had vast reserves of young men to throw into the battle, but every single European country – save for Russia – was stretched to the limit in human and material resources.

Bartosz elbowed him and Peter looked up. The short impromptu performance had ended and they were supposed to clap. Someone started singing the national anthem, *"Jeszcze Polska Nie Zginęła"*, Poland Is Not Yet Lost, and everyone joined in. Men stood up and filled the barracks with gritty determination. Despite the hardships they would never give up hope of making it home one day.

"It looks like the Germans are gaining ground again," someone said into the silence after the singing had ebbed.

"Pray to God it won't be the Russians who liberate us." A shudder went through Bartosz and Peter wondered what he'd been subjected to in having to fight alongside the Red Army.

"Nah. We're good," another soldier said. "Fallingbostel is deep in the Western part of the North German Plain. The Western Allies will get here first."

"But with them getting engaged in the Ardennes the juggernaut of the Red Army might reach us first, and then we're all toast."

"Come on, they can't do anything worse than the Germans have been doing to us," someone from the back of the barracks threw into the conversation.

"Are you stupid? When they liberate their own nationals from the POW camps they send them to Siberian Gulags for cowardice before the enemy or collaboration. In Stalin's eyes every soldier who didn't die fighting is a traitor." Bartosz's voice turned bitter. "I've been there and seen it. And now that the Soviets have claimed their stake in Poland, they'll do the same with us."

Before a dispute could break out, Peter appeased the men. "It won't do any of us any good to speculate. There's nothing we can do either way. Our job is to hang on and survive."

"See my family again."

"Kiss my wife," Tomasz, a recent transfer from another POW camp, said.

"How long?" the man next to him asked.

"How long what?"

"Without sex?"

"Oh." Tomasz wrinkled his nose, calculating. "Two years and seven months."

"That's nothing," an older prisoner added. "Five years and two months. Since bloody Hitler bloody invaded our country."

"You've been here for five years?" Tomasz's jaw fell to the floor as he stared at the other man.

"Not here. I've been to more camps and work parties than I can count with my two hands. And each is worse than the one before…"

"Let's not dwell on morose thoughts," Peter said and cast a pleading glance at the chaplain amongst them. The chaplain stepped forward and said a prayer over them all, talking about how God would reward the righteous one day and how evil couldn't last forever.

It was a miserable solace.

CHAPTER 23: ANNA

After her shift at the Charité Anna rushed home to bring her mother and sister the good news.

"Mutter, Ursula! You have to hear this!"

Both women appeared in the hallway, their faces lined with worry. Mutter looked tired in her mended black dress. The long shifts at the ammunition factory she'd been forced to work, combined with the nightly air raids, were taking a toll on her.

"What's wrong," Ursula asked, holding Evie on her hip.

"Nothing." Anna grinned. "I'm bringing good news, very good news."

"The war's over?" Hope lit up in Ursula's face.

"Not that good." Anna thought for a moment how to best break the news. Ursula knew about Stan's and Anna's role in saving him from the camp, but Mutter didn't. "So there's this Polish soldier at the hospital…"

"An enemy soldier? Isn't that dangerous for the nurses?" Mutter asked.

"No, Mutter. In fact, he's a kind person and…he knows Richard!"

"Richard?" Mutter and Ursula yelped in unison. "As in our Richard?"

"Yes. Can you believe it?" Again, she paused for a moment, considering how she could spoon-feed her mother with the details. "Apparently Richard is hiding on the farm of a friend of his. Richard is alive!"

Her mother squinted her eyes and Anna knew she wasn't buying into the story. "So, how exactly did you and this prisoner get to talk about your missing brother?"

"Well," Anna ran a hand across her straight blonde hair, seeking help from Ursula. But her sister only gave her an apologetic shrug. When Mutter was on a quest to get to the bottom of things, nothing and no one could stop her.

"Well?"

"Since it was Christmas, I showed him some family photographs and—"

"You did what? Sharing family memories with an enemy?" Mutter scolded her.

"He's not an enemy."

"He's not? Last time I checked the Poles were our enemies. What aren't you telling me?" Mutter insisted.

Anna didn't have to answer the question because the door opened and Jan came inside carrying heavy bags laden with groceries.

"I got almost everything that's on our ration cards, but I had to queue at three different stores." He beamed with pride and then tugged at Anna's sleeve. "Can I visit Uncle Stan again, please?"

Anna felt the blood fleeing from her head at the same

time as her mother furrowed her brow. "Who is Uncle Stan?"

Jan's childlike innocence didn't allow him to understand the brewing thunderstorm he'd caused with his remark and he gleefully answered, "He's my dad's brother and he's a patient in Anna's hospital."

"Would you be a darling and store the groceries in the pantry, Jan?" Mutter asked, before she gave Anna a dark stare.

"I'll go and help him," Ursula added, fleeing the room and the upcoming scolding.

"I reckon this Uncle Stan is the Polish soldier you just mentioned?" Mutter's voice dripped icicles.

"Yes, Mutter." Anna lowered her head.

"And you somehow forgot to tell me this detail?"

"I didn't want to upset you," Anna whispered.

"I'm upset. Very much so. And not about some enemy soldier, but about the fact that my own daughter is keeping information from me and lying to me."

Anna nodded. There wasn't really that much to say. "I apologize. It was wrong not to tell you. I did it to keep you safe. The less you know…"

"…the better it is for me. I know all this and I don't agree with it. You and Ursula have brought enough trouble into this house and…" Mutter raised a hand to her chest. "God knows I have raised you to be loyal and decent women."

"Mutter, please. You did raise us to have moral values. But," she lowered her voice to a whisper, "Hitler is trampling those values with his feet and we must stand up to do the right thing. Stan is Peter's brother and would have died in the camp, so I persuaded Professor Scherer to have him transferred to the Charité." Anna did not elaborate on the lies she'd had to use to make this transfer happen. "Fact is, Stan has last seen our brother near Lodz less than half a year ago. He even helped him to escape to a friend's farm, posing as a Pole."

"I'm getting too old for this," Mutter said. "I just hope we all survive this god-awful war."

Sometime later, Ursula and Anna sat in the kitchen drinking *Ersatzkaffee*.

"I never get used to this stuff. It simply tastes awful." Ursula sighed.

"The plan to make Germany great again didn't turn out so great, did it? We don't even have coffee anymore. Or fresh fruit, or enough food, or clothes…or shoes," she said, thinking about Jan's toes wedged in his too-small shoes.

"When will it finally end?" Ursula asked, spoon-feeding Evie with mashed potatoes.

"I wish I knew the answer."

"It's frustrating. We're sitting here, waiting for what? Conditions are deteriorating faster than Berlin's ruins when the bombs are falling."

The baby spit out mashed potatoes and Anna hurried to wipe the mess away. "Evie is the sweetest baby I know."

"For now," Ursula agreed, worry evident in her voice.

Anna grew somber and looked her sister in the eye. "You need to consider leaving Berlin."

"You know I can't do that," Ursula argued.

"Can't or won't? They are very different things. I understood you wanting to stay here before the birth, but now with Pfarrer Bernau gone, and the *Ivan* approaching… you need to consider her safety."

"The Russians are still far away…" Ursula protested.

"They are coming closer every day. And you heard the stories. They stop at nothing. Not even baby girls." Anna couldn't bring herself to pronounce the word rape. It held too many awful memories. Memories she never wanted to revisit in her entire life again.

"I can't leave," Ursula repeated, even as she paled and hugged Evie close. "Tom said he would come back…"

"When the war's over," Anna reminded her. "He'll return when things have settled down and he'll find you. I'm not saying you need to stay out of Berlin forever, just until the war is over. Do it for Evie."

"Where would I go?" Ursula asked, even though they'd had this discussion multiple times.

"Back to Bavaria with Aunt Lydia. You know she didn't want you to return here in the first place. Berlin is not the best place to be right now." Anna shuddered. Even if she wanted to, she wouldn't be allowed to leave the capital. Hitler denied even the remotest possibility that Germany might lose this war. As a nurse she was considered indispensable to the war effort.

"But Tom…"

"*Schwesterherz*, I'll have to stay here to the very end. My work at the hospital and Stan…what I'm saying is that I'll be around to tell Tom where you are if he shows up."

Ursula gave a doubtful nod and took a sip from her *Ersatzkaffee*. "What about Jan?"

"What about me?" Jan asked, appearing in the doorway to the kitchen.

"Aunt Ursula is going to take Evie to a farm in Bavaria while this war comes to an end. I want you to go with her," Anna said after giving him a once-over.

"No. I'm not going." He put his feet hip-wide apart and pushed out his chest. A wave of nostalgia swept over Anna.

He looked just like his father.

"Jan, it would be safer…"

"You womenfolk need a man in the house. And Uncle Stan..." His glacial blue eyes sparkled their defiance. If the situation weren't so dire, Anna would laugh at his antics. She sent Ursula a glance, thankful for the way they could communicate without words, when her sister nodded and said, "I'd better put Evie to bed."

Anna pointed at the vacant chair. "Sit down."

Nobody had ever taught her how to debate a twelve-year-old. When she was his age it was absolutely unheard of to even question the wishes of your parents. She shook her head. Things had changed so much in ten years, it was unbelievable.

But Jan didn't sit on the chair, instead he snaked his arms around her and hugged her tight. "Please don't make me leave. Please? I promise to be a good boy always."

As her heart constricted, words failed her. "Alright. You can stay here with me."

Not making Jan's safety her top priority might come back to haunt her, but she couldn't deny having him around brought her joy and comfort. Together they'd withstand the anxiety and sorrow until Peter returned.

CHAPTER 24: PETER

Several days after Christmas, other prisoners brought the news that all female Home Army members who'd been held in a separate area of the camp were going to be transferred to the camp in Oberlangen, near the border with the Netherlands.

"Why on earth would the Nazis do this?" Peter asked. The German resources were stretched thin already so why start moving prisoners around?

"Not sure," the other man said, "but I've heard that Fallingbostel will be closed down."

Peter gasped at the impact of this information. Thousands upon thousands of debilitated prisoners in bad physical shape would be on the move to God only knew where.

"Apparently the Nazis expect the final battle to take place right here in the middle of the North German Plain, so they need us out of the way. Afraid we might take up the fight and reinforce the Allied troops should push come to shove."

But as always, the flurry of rumors slowed down and senseless activities came to a halt. A week after the women soldiers left, everyone else remained, toiling as usual. Just when Peter forgot about the alleged plan to close down the camp, five hundred Home Army officers were called up during roll call. They stood for hours in the biting cold January frost, fearing the worst.

"Everyone on the trains," the guards yelled. "*Schnell! Schnell!*"

"Where are we going?" Peter asked, but instead of an answer, the butt of a rifle pushed him forward. Would his worst nightmares come true and they'd be shipped to one of the extermination camps?

Peter stumbled behind the others to the nearby ramp, where they were shoved into boxcars, fifty men each. The five-day journey was one of the worst experiences of his entire life, and he was amazed to still be alive when the doors finally opened and a rough voice shouted, "*Raus! Schnell!*"

He followed the orders, climbing across the corpses of fellows who'd succumbed to thirst, hunger or frailty during the journey. He never thought he'd one day wish himself back at Stalag XIB in Fallingbostel. But exactly this was his first thought when he was marched into the new camp.

It was severely overcrowded, even before accommodating the influx of new prisoners. Typhus, dysentery and every other imaginable sickness ran rampant amongst the prisoners and the guards didn't show a modicum of compassion, unlike some of the guards in Fallingbostel. The smallest sliver of hope flickered when he found Bartosz, who'd survived the hellish trip in another boxcar.

He sank to the ground, greedily shoving snow into his mouth to quench the insupportable thirst that had plagued him since he got onto the cattle wagon five days earlier.

"Where are we?" Peter asked one of the resident inmates.

"In hell," the man said, not even bothering to look up. The sunken cheeks and empty gaze betrayed his state of mind.

"Gross Born, Pomerania, but hell describes it better. Make yourself comfortable," the man next to him said with a grand gesture encompassing the camp.

Peter swallowed hard. Gross Born was deep in the East near the border with Poland. *So near to home and yet so far.* But the approaching Red Army and what they might do to Home Army members worried him even more. Based on previous experiences, nothing nice could be expected.

"Why on earth did they send us here when they've been moving lots of prisoners West?" Peter whispered to Bartosz.

"Who knows?" Bartosz shrugged. "Grasping what goes on in the mind of a Nazi is beyond me."

Peter sneered. His friend was right. Logic and reason didn't mesh well with Nazi ideology. All he could do was settle into conditions even worse than before and hope to live another day.

Winter had come with full force, and everyone agreed it was the coldest since time immemorial. Peter was thankful for the warm felt boots and the greatcoat he'd snatched from a dead comrade before the corpse had been discarded in the morning.

Man-high snow covered the country and at night the temperatures fell to minus twenty-five degrees centigrade outside, and it wasn't much warmer in the unheated barracks either. Two years ago someone had constructed a radio from smuggled parts, which had since proven a valuable source of information.

The Vistula Lagoon and the Gdansk Bay in the Baltic Sea were frozen over and despite an official prohibition against fleeing and showing cowardice before the enemy, every day hundreds of Germans from East Prussia, Silesia and Pomerania left everything behind and started their long trek westward into Germany.

"Serves them right," one man said.

"If they hadn't committed all those cruel crimes, they wouldn't have to fear anything," another one chimed in.

"I'll squash any bloody German I encounter between my thumbs like an ant."

"Not all Germans are bad," Peter objected.

"What do you know? Are you a fucking collaborator?" several men accused him, ready to lynch him.

"He's not. He fought in the Warsaw Uprising, but if it weren't for the kindness of a German nurse, his brother would be long dead," Bartosz came to his aid.

Peter quieted, but guilt and doubt seeped into his bones. Was he a traitor to his nation for loving a German woman?

Day after day news about the approaching Red Army trickled in; it was only a matter of time until they'd be liberated. Even Peter started to yearn for the hated Russians to show up at the gates of the camp. He thought his life couldn't possibly get any worse.

It could.

CHAPTER 25: STAN

In January 1945 Anna stood beside Professor Scherer and a circle of doctors. Stan didn't like the expression on her face one bit. This morning she'd come to change his bandages, and the stench of rotting flesh combined with the dark green pus seeping from the wound had put a frown on her otherwise beautiful face. This woman simply couldn't hide her emotions.

"Herr Zdanek," one of the doctors said with a grave voice, "your leg is gangrenous."

Gangrenous? Surely there was something they could do about it.

"We have run out of treatments to try. And at this point there's nothing else we can do. The miraculous drug penicillin might have helped, but despite all our efforts we haven't been able to secure a supply."

Stan wondered at the truth of the words or whether they wouldn't bother to go to the trouble for a prisoner of war, even though he allegedly was the godson of Churchill.

"What I want to say is that the infection is beginning to spread to the surrounding tissues, and we need to remove it."

Remove the infection. Fine. Why are they making such a fuss about it?

It wasn't as if the doctors had consulted or even explained the treatments to him earlier. A horrible suspicion crept into his thoughts and he looked at Anna again. But she averted her eyes.

"So remove the infection," Stan said.

The doctor gazed at Professor Scherer for help and the uneasy feeling in the pit of Stan's stomach intensified.

"What Doctor Huber meant to say is we will have to amputate your leg to save your life."

"You want to cut off my leg?" Stan hissed in shock.

Anna stepped forward, offering him what compassion she could. "It's the only way to keep you alive. There's no way to heal the tissues once gangrene sets in."

"I'll arrange it for this afternoon," Professor Scherer stated and fled the room, the other doctors trailing behind

Anna lingered in the room. When the doctors left, she stepped beside his bed, sorrow etched deeply into her expression.

"Is this really the only way? I'll be a useless cripple. A burden for my family." He closed his eyes for a moment afraid he'd shed a tear if he kept looking at her. Who would care for him? Anna? His brother? His sister? They had enough on their hands without the encumbrance of a cripple in the family.

Anna clasped his hand for a moment before she met his

eyes. "This is not the end of the world. You can walk with crutches. But you'll be alive to do it."

"Better to let me die." Stan flopped back against the pillow turning his head away. He wouldn't be a real man anymore without his leg. He'd be a shamed and ridiculed good-for-nothing.

"Stan. Please look at me. You're such a strong man; you can master this. Even without your leg, you'll still be strong and have much to offer this world. Your family loves you. Jan needs you."

Stan scoffed. "Nobody needs a cripple. Leave me alone."

Anna's mouth opened, but no words came out and she bowed her head with a sad smile before she left his bedside. Stan didn't care. He wouldn't be a burden to anyone. If it were up to him, they could just let him rot away. But if he died, Peter's sacrifice would be in vain.

And that burdened his soul more than anything else.

Could he really betray his brother by not embracing the chance to live?

In the afternoon a tousled mop of dark hair peeked inside the room.

"Hello, Jan," Stan said.

"Anna told me they have to cut off your leg." The boy came to Stan's bed.

Stan grimaced. "They should just let me die."

"No! You can't say that, Uncle Stan." Jan's eyes widened in horror. "You can't leave me alone."

You're not alone. You still have Anna and her family, Stan wanted to answer but thought better of it. He gave a heavy sigh. "I won't be of much use to anyone…"

"That's not true." Jan violently shook his head. "See how fast I can run with one leg." He hopped across the room on one leg, making Stan chuckle.

"See? You just have to exercise a bit and you can be even faster than I am."

If only it were that easy. Stan didn't have the heart to disappoint the eager boy with adult worries. Hopping fast across the room didn't make one a man. Being able to work and support his family did. Who would employ a cripple without formal education? At twenty-six years of age all he'd learned was how to tend a farm and how to fight.

With only one leg he wouldn't be able to do either one. Instead of one day having his own family he'd live his life at the charity of relatives who'd kindly shelter and feed him. Thanks, but no thanks.

Jan returned to his side and wrapped his skinny arms around Stan. "Anna said you promised my dad that you'd take care of her and me until he returns."

"I did," Stan said through gritted teeth. Obviously Anna had primed the boy.

"And promises have to be kept, right?"

"Right."

His naïve gaze stared Stan down. "But you can't do this when you're dead."

"Right."

Jan raised his head, his glacial blue eyes shiny. "So you let them do whatever they need to keep you alive. Promise?"

"Alright." Stan sighed. He was powerless against the determination of his nephew.

"Swear it," Jan demanded.

"I swear I will do everything to stay alive." They shook hands and Stan managed a faint smile. "Are you satisfied now?"

"Very much. I'll come and visit you every day until you can leave the hospital."

Another thought sent shivers down Stan's spine. Even if he completely healed and was allowed to leave the hospital, where would they send him? He was still a prisoner of war, albeit a very privileged one.

Later, when Jan had left, Stan relapsed into his tortured thoughts. Anna meant well and her visits were welcome, but the bright spot in his existence was Jan. Every day Jan's energy, determination and zest for life amazed Stan.

After all Jan had been through, he should be broken. Desolate. Terrified. But he was nothing like that. If Jan could be a happy boy after his awful ordeal, maybe Stan himself could experience joy again even after having his leg amputated?

When they came for him in the afternoon, he wasn't so sure anymore.

CHAPTER 26: PETER

Peter picked his feet up and put them down again, taking one step after another automatically, without wasting energy for anything except the movement of his legs. Every step sent a low burn through his soles, the raw pain moving up his calves, building, burning stronger as it swept up his thighs. His hips ached and tingled with an intense agony he hadn't known existed. Every nerve ending shot pain into every last inch of his tormented body as he trudged forward – one step at a time.

His big toe bumped against the confinement of the too-small felt boots and he wished it would puncture a hole in them, despite the freezing cold temperatures. He didn't know which was worse, frostbitten toes or swollen, glowing toes.

On January 21, a mere nine days after his arrival in Gross Born, the Nazis had forced him onto the move again, this time on foot. They evacuated the entire camp, except for the men who couldn't walk. Five thousand miserable souls on a death march. Peter had no idea where they were headed; the only thing he knew for sure was the direction. Due west.

"Isn't it ironic? We're walking back to where we came from just a week ago," Bartosz groaned.

"Hmm." Peter didn't want to waste energy on talking. Food was almost non-existent and they'd been on the move for eight days without pause. Walking from sunrise to sundown, huddling together in ditches from sundown to sunrise.

Walk. Sleep. Walk. Sleep.

His entire life had been reduced to the movement of setting one foot in front of the other. In the distance he heard artillery fire. No doubt the Russians approaching. They passed deserted villages, and sometimes stopped to sleep in the forsaken buildings or to rummage for food. Rarely were they successful. The only thing in abundance was snow to melt and quench their thirst.

Columns of civilians passed them, fleeing with all the belongings they could carry. Some had handcarts, horse-drawn carriages, bicycles and even prams, but most of them walked. They looked almost as miserable as the prisoners. The only difference that they weren't beaten or shot, and looked comparatively well-fed.

Peter didn't envy them, but he would have traded places with every single one of the refugees without a second thought. During the first days of the march, when he'd still had enough energy to think, he'd wondered whether those left in the camp had been dealt the better cards. Being liberated by the detested Russians suddenly didn't seem as bad. Even a shot in the back of the head held a certain allure.

Some of his comrades went for just that. They fell out of step, using their last ounce of strength to run a few steps away from the column.

"Stop! Anhalten!" the guards would yell, but the desperate prisoner continued on, surely awaiting his quick end. A shot would be discharged with heartless cruelty, a bullet would whizz through the air, and the man would fall. Swiftly and without a sound, soaking the immaculate white snow with red blood.

Only thoughts of Anna and Janusz prevented Peter from doing the same. And his friend Bartosz by his side. The proverb of shared sorrow definitely held a lot of truth. With Bartosz he shared what little food they found, murmured rallying cries to hold out, and huddled together at night against the bone-chilling cold. Every morning, some comrades had turned into icicles, frozen to the ground, as their emaciated bodies had nothing left to resist the brutal winter nights.

"Aufstehen! Los!" the guards yelled every morning, counting the dead and the living to make sure the numbers added up. No prisoner was allowed to slip through the cracks and be left behind. But this morning they were three prisoners short. They counted again. And again. Same result.

The guard in charge pursed his lips in an annoyed expression and ordered his men to set up three machine guns at the perimeter. Then he shouted, "If you care anything about your comrades, come out now or I will give the order to fire!"

Peter felt an icy hand grab his heart, effectively paralyzing him, while his mind rushed with a million thoughts. He stared into the cold muzzle of the mounted machine guns wishing he could kiss Anna one last time. Hold his son again and tell him how much he loved him. How would the two of them cope when they found out? If they ever found out...Or would he be yet another missing soul never to be found again, buried in a mass grave for the unknown soldier?

Cold seeped into his bones and he glanced to his side, seeing the same fatalism in Bartosz's eyes. In the complete silence he heard the nerve-racking sound of the machines guns being charged. Peter stood helpless, his hands hanging by his side, hoping and praying that the missing three would give up and save their comrades' lives.

The seconds trickled by when finally the heavenly sound of a Polish voice came across the field in a thick accent, "Hold your fire. We are coming out."

Relief washed over Peter's limbs as he realized he wouldn't be a hapless soul caught in the crossfire. He stared at the three escapees, sure that, right then and there, the mob would have dealt with them, if the Germans hadn't frog-marched them away.

"What gall," Bartosz whispered. Everyone knew that reprisals were harsh for attempts to escape.

"Gall or desperation."

"*Schnell!*" The guards used their rifle butts with abandon on anyone not falling into step with the column fast enough.

With every aching step Peter fought the urge to give up, to slide down into the cold snow and never open his eyes again. But the thought of Anna propelled him forward. With each step westward he reduced the distance between them. If he survived this deathly march through ice and wind, if he survived long enough for the Allies East or West to reach his position, he might see her again.

For many reasons he preferred to be liberated by the Western Allies, but right now he'd welcome Stalin's army with open arms if only they'd put an end to his ordeal. The war was about to end. That much was for sure. He just had to hang on for a little bit more.

One step at a time.

After two weeks they crossed the Oder River and marched on. The endless cold, snow and ice took its toll on everyone, even on the guards. Tempers were short, desperation rampant.

The prisoner column dwindled by the day, but each morning they were forced on the march again. Many times Peter thought it wasn't humanly possible to continue walking, but each time he gathered his inner strength around him like a cloak and proved himself wrong.

"Ouch!" Bartosz yelled and fell to the ground.

"Get up," Peter rushed to his side, shoving and pushing to get his friend upright again.

"I…can't…I…" Bartosz pressed out between gritted teeth.

"You have to!"

Bartosz did his best, but the pained groan he released when putting weight on his ankle indicated it was severely twisted or even broken.

"Here, lean on me," Peter said, putting Bartosz's arm around his own shoulders. Even though his friend was nothing more than a bag of bones, the additional burden weighed down heavily on Peter, who looked like a skeleton himself.

The men in front of them and in back of them closed up their ranks to hide the fact that Peter was helping Bartosz continue to walk. That night, Peter packed snow around Bartosz's swollen ankle, which had taken on a nasty black and green color.

From a superficial examination it didn't seem to be broken, but Peter was no doctor and neither was any other prisoner. Peter touched the hot skin in the most delicate way possible, and yet Bartosz winced in pain.

"You'll see, it'll be better in the morning," Peter said, not really believing his own words.

The next morning Bartosz's ankle had doubled in size. "I don't know how I can walk all day."

"We'll make a splint to stabilize it," Peter suggested and some other comrades started looking for sticks beneath the snow. Somehow they managed to make a splint from sturdy sticks, wrapping them up with strips of material torn from the bottom of Peter's shirt.

Bartosz grimaced in agony with every step, but at least he could get up and walk again. They got into the head of the formation right away to allow them to slowly slink to the back throughout the day and thus keep up with the rest.

Snow had fallen most of the night and the path turned slick as the temperature continued to drop. They came to a slight decline, where Bartosz slipped, taking Peter and several others tumbling to the ground.

Before Peter could assess what exactly had happened,

one of the guards surged to their side, rifle pointing at them, "*Aufstehen. Schnell.*"

Prisoners scrambled to their feet, the guard shoving them forward with rifle thumps at their backs. Peter went on all fours and was trying to help Bartosz up when he sensed cold metal in his neck.

Every tiny hair on his body stood on end as he listened to the guard's voice saying, "Get up. Now."

His heart shattered into a thousand pieces as he raised his hands and stood, sending his friend an apologetic glance, whispering, "Forgive me."

Neither Peter nor Bartosz had any illusions about what would happen. They'd seen it more times than they cared to remember.

"Move." A hard push between his shoulder blades almost sent Peter tumbling to the ground, but he managed to put a foot forward and start walking, closing up with the moving file.

"Now you." Peter heard the guard yell at Bartosz, but he kept his eyes trained forward, not wanting to see or know.

A scream of anguish tore through the crystal-clear air as Bartosz tried to get up, followed by a dull thump. A shot rang out, echoing through Peter's head. He swirled around, ready to lunge at the guard and rip the heart from his chest, but two comrades held his arms.

"Don't be dumb. Your friend's dead."

As the truth of the words pierced his soul, a wave of helplessness flowed over him. There was nothing he could do. The fight seeped from his body and he became limp, automatically following the commands of his comrades to keep walking.

Bartosz was dead and nobody seemed to care.

Blazing hatred fueled his steps, the yearning to survive and avenge Bartosz's death bubbling up like a cauldron of rage. He'd make them pay. Every last damn Nazi would pay for this.

CHAPTER 27: ANNA

February 1945

Since she'd found out that a group of five hundred Polish officers, including Peter, had been transferred to the Oflag Gross Born, deep in Pomerania, worry and guilt consumed Anna.

Obviously she couldn't voice her concerns to Professor Scherer or she'd already have asked him what dumb pencil pusher had decided to move Home Army prisoners into the den of the lion. Everyone, even the dumbest Nazi, knew how Stalin's army treated the Poles who'd been fighting for their country. But maybe that was exactly their plan, getting rid of the prisoners without even lifting a finger.

She carefully investigated and much to her horror found out that the entire camp at Gross Born had been evacuated and all prisoners put on an excruciating march to Sandbostel, some five hundred miles away.

Her heart squeezed painfully when she thought of Peter

trudging day after day through snow, wind and ice. She knew enough to not delude herself into believing he'd be properly clothed and fed to withstand such conditions.

While most of the Nazis Professor Scherer socialized with admitted the need to evacuate the prisoner of war population into the West, they also agreed – behind closed doors – that the evacuation was riddled with disorganization, confusion and a lack of planning. Some even went so far as to secretly argue that none of these prisoners were in fit condition to march. Heartless cruelty and death marches were some of the words uttered, although nobody dared to say them in public.

This knowledge didn't help to soothe Anna's worries or alleviate her guilt. She should have insisted on bringing Peter with her, should have come up with another plan to rescue him, should have…

She hadn't told a single soul about her torment. Now that Ursula and the baby had travelled to the countryside she had nobody to confide in, since she didn't want to put the burden of guilt on Stan, who grew grumpier by the day. Neither did she want Jan to know his father was forced on a death march as long as even the slightest hope remained that Peter would return alive.

After a long shift at the hospital she walked home, snowflakes fluttering down in the evening darkness. In the distance she heard the low rumble of planes and just like that the repressed emotions of so many months broke through like water bursting a dam. She stumbled over to sit on a heap of rubble and bawled.

She sat there for a long time…lost in her grief and crying for the man she loved so much. The tears freezing on her cheeks, she cried for the thousands upon thousands of prisoners on the march like him, for the hundreds of thousands tortured, miserable souls captive in the concentrations camps. For the millions of lives lost, for the sacrifices made, the men maimed.

Shadows of darkness hovered over her, seemingly waiting to swoop down and attack, to suck the spirit out of her and leave her slumped, lifeless. Another corpse amongst the millions of corpses littering the earth across Europe.

"Woman, you're going to freeze to death," someone said and she recognized an old man with only one arm who'd been a patient of hers.

"I'm fine. Just leave me to die," she murmured, closing her eyes as a second wave of tears flooded her eyes.

"I'm not going to do any such thing, Schwester Anna," he said, recognizing her as well. "You're the nurse who saved my life and I'll return the favor now." He yanked her up, gripping her elbow and dragging her behind. "Where do you live?"

She gave him the address, not caring about anything right now. Darkness had swallowed her and she feared she'd never feel happiness again in her life should Peter die on this senseless march. Everything became fuzzy, and blissful silence engulfed her.

The next morning, steps from outside woke Anna and she jerked from her bed, disoriented. Her gaze fell on the sleeping Jan by her side. Bits and pieces of the previous evening returned. The kind man leading her home. Her apartment building. Stairs upon stairs. The aghast face of her mother. Hot liquid running down her throat. The intense pain when her feet and hands started to thaw.

"Darling, do you want tea?" her mother asked, peeking inside the room.

"Yes, Mutter. I'll be right out." She slipped into her morning robe and slippers and met her mother in the kitchen, taking a steaming cup of herb tea from her hands.

"You gave me quite a fright last night," Mutter said, her lips pursed.

"I'm sorry…I was…overwhelmed."

Her mother nodded with understanding eyes. Every woman was overwhelmed. They had lost their sons, husbands, brothers and fathers, and now they were waiting with bated breath for the Red Army to arrive. For centuries past, the women of the enemy had been the ultimate reward for the victorious army. It wouldn't be any different this time. They all knew the fate that would await them at the hands of the Russian soldiers.

And despite the propaganda touted by Goebbels's ministry, no woman in the capital believed that Stalin would never set foot into Berlin. Not anymore.

Anna gave a deep sigh. "I should get dressed and return to the hospital."

"There's a letter for you," Mutter said, handing her a big white envelope that read *Feldpostbrief* and showed the official Wehrmacht stamp.

Anna took the letter and turned it around, deciphering her sister Lotte's army identification number. Lotte worked under the fake identity of Alexandra Wagner as *Wehrmachthelferin,* secretly spying for the British. Anna's hands trembled even as her mother said, "It's Lotte's handwriting, which is a good sign."

The dead can't write.

Anna carefully opened the perforation and unfolded the letter, scanning the words before she read them aloud to her mother.

My dear friend Anna,

Thank you so much for your Christmas wishes which I received two weeks late, because we had moved to another garrison. I am not allowed to tell you the exact location, except that I'm still in Norway. But rest assured, I'm well cared for and the Norwegian people are very nice. I don't speak a word of their language, but most of them speak some German or English.

You can imagine how grateful I am now for the little English I learned at school. It does help when going to the grocery store or a hairdresser.

Do you remember my friend, Gerlinde? She's deployed together with me and it's a relief to have a good friend like her when you're so far away from home. Unfortunately, she has not heard from her family in East Prussia, but we are all confident that nothing bad happened to them.

Anna's hand sunk to her lap. Obviously Lotte had been writing this letter as much for the censors as for her sister. The stories from the refugees pouring into Germany from

East Prussia, Silesia and Pomerania didn't justify believing that nothing bad happened to them.

I hope you, your sister and your mother are fine and don't have to suffer too much from the Allied air raids. Has cousin Jan adapted to living with your family? Please tell me everything about your family, as you're my only link to Germany.

Here, we're all eagerly awaiting the wonder weapon to end the war, which our Führer says is only a matter of time.

On that part Anna agreed with Hitler: the war would end soon. But she didn't see eye to eye with him on the outcome. A German victory was as improbable as Hitler showing compassion toward a Jew.

It is with great sorrow I have to tell you that Johann—

"Who is Johann?" asked her mother with a raised brow.

Anna crunched her nose, not sure what she could reveal. Leutnant Johann Hauser was Lotte's boyfriend, whom she'd met during her last deployment in Warsaw. Mutter would definitely not approve of her eighteen-year-old daughter having a boyfriend, much less one ten years older. But then, Mutter had almost never approved of anything the free-spirited and strong-willed nestling of the family had done.

"He's the man who arranged false papers for Jan," Anna said, telling part of the truth.

Mutter thinned her lips into a line, obviously filling the blanks with her own assumptions.

—has been captured by the Red Army near Warsaw and is now a prisoner of war. This is all I know about his whereabouts. Please keep him in your prayers.

I'm sending you my very best wishes and hope to see you again one day.

Love,

Alexandra

"I'm glad she's still in Norway," Mutter said after a while.

"Yes, that's probably one of the safest places in all of Europe right now. I have heard they've never seen fighting nor air raids up there," Anna answered with a wistful smile.

"Write your sister not to return to Berlin if she can avoid it. She'll be much better off if she can experience the end of the war in Norway."

"I will." Anna peered at her mother and really saw her for the first time in a while. Her hair had become gray and wrinkles had been etched into her beautiful face, a permanent frown of sorrow cutting deep into her forehead. In a sudden burst of emotion she wrapped her arms around her mother and said, "Everything will be fine."

"Off course it will be." Mutter dabbed at her eyes, pretending to believe Anna's words.

"I have to leave. See you tonight," Anna said and returned to her room, waking Jan with a kiss to the top of his head. Now that Ursula was gone and she and Mutter worked all day, he bore the burden of queuing up for rations and whatever else was needed.

"Can I visit Uncle Stan this afternoon?" Jan asked before she left.

"If you are careful to sneak in when the doctors don't see you and never speak a single word in Polish with him," she warned him.

"I promise," he vowed, beaming his brightest smile at her, and suddenly the day didn't seem so bleak anymore.

"Love you, Jan. Take care and I'll see you in the afternoon." She ruffled his hair, looking at his glacial blue eyes that reminded her so much of his father. She had to stay strong. For Jan.

At the hospital she visited Stan, who was even grumpier than usual. His stump had healed very well, but mentally and emotionally he worsened by the day and she feared he might do something stupid.

CHAPTER 28: STAN

More than a month ago, he'd woken after the surgery only half a man. A cripple. His hopes, his future, everything shattered. They had destroyed his manhood, the ability to take care of himself or anyone else.

Why didn't they let me die? Peter should have saved himself and not me. I never deserved it. I should be where Jarek is, dead and dumped into a ditch.

His hand fingered the stump. It was well-healed and they'd taken the bandages away, but he refused to look at the *thing* that hung from his hip. That useless stump of itching and burning flesh.

Anna assured him it looked good, but she was a nurse. She had lied to make him feel better. He'd seen the disgust in Jan's eyes when the boy had first caught a glimpse of the fiery-red skin with the large and ugly scar.

No woman would ever find him attractive again. The thought stabbed at his heart. He was so young, and yet he'd never again be able to enjoy lying with a woman. He'd have to finish his days on earth celibate. *I should become a Catholic priest.*

Roaring laughter escaped his throat at the thought of a priest who'd known nothing but war since becoming an adult, killing more men than he wanted to remember.

"Are you alright, Herr Zdanek?" The peachy blonde nurse poked her head inside the room.

He'd tried flirting with her before, but she was immune to his charms, pretending to be engaged. But he knew better. She was appalled by him. Everyone was appalled by him.

When she left the room, he sank against the pillow, not able to look any longer at the flatness of the sheet where his leg should be. He closed his eyes and let out a loud cry, tears threatening to spill. He stared at the ceiling until dark shadows danced in front of his eyes from the strain.

A creaking noise made him jerk his head toward the door.

"Hi, Uncle Stan, how are you?" Jan slid into the room with a bright smile on his face. But not even Jan's presence could lighten his mood today.

"Bad."

"But Anna told me your leg healed well." Jan approached his bed, his brows knit together in confusion.

"I don't have my leg anymore. They took it away, if you don't remember," Stan growled.

Jan made a face as if he'd hit him and a sliver of guilt penetrated Stan's brain, but he brushed it off. *I'm the miserable fellow here, not him. He still has both of his legs.*

"They should have let me die. It would have been better for everyone."

The boy's face fell into a grimace of pain, fighting against erupting tears as he crawled up onto the other side of the bed. "No, you can't die. I need you."

"Nobody needs me." Stan wasn't in the mood for a hug and turned away, saying, "Go. You have better things to do than visit with a cripple."

Jan swallowed, but didn't say another word as he slid from the bed and left the room. Stan's feeling of guilt intensified, but again he brushed it off. It was for the best. Jan shouldn't have to feel obligated to visit a useless uncle confined to his bed.

In the afternoon Anna entered the room, carrying a huge package beneath her arm. He waited to find out what she had planned this time. She was continually trying to cheer him up and couldn't seem to understand that he didn't want to be cheered up. He simply wanted to be left alone.

"How are you, Stan?" she asked with a smile, looking immaculate as always in her nurse's uniform with her straight blonde hair tied up into a knot at the nape of her neck.

He answered with a growl.

She cocked her head, saying, "I see. Your usual grumpy self."

"I have every right to be grumpy."

"Your scar has healed well, and it's about time you stop wallowing in self-pity and start living again."

"There's nothing worth living for me."

He could see how she took a deep breath to stay calm

and even managed to keep the smile on her face. She might have fooled anyone, but by now he knew her well enough to notice the dangerous glint in her eyes.

"Professor Scherer told me you're well enough to be released from the hospital. He's arranging for a place for you in one of the better prison hospitals, where you'll spend the remainder of the war."

"And that's supposed to be good news why?" Stan fired back.

With the patience of an angel she explained to him that he was still a prisoner of war and couldn't be set free, but that the nearby Reservelazarett where he was destined to go was a small prison hospital with dedicated doctors and nurses for VIP patients.

He didn't care. Should they dump him in the garbage and let him rot alive, he didn't give one damn.

"Stan, I have a gift for you," she said, extending her hands with the package.

He refused to take the package so she walked closer and laid it on his lap.

"Open it," she insisted, a slight tremor of annoyance mixing into her cheerful tone.

Stan sighed, knowing she wouldn't quit badgering him until he did what she wanted. He tore it open. Anger flared up in his chest, sending a violent burning sensation into every cell of his body as he stared at the monstrosity on his lap.

"How dare you!" he yelled at her. "How dare you bring that...that...thing in here and think it makes everything better?" He picked up the prosthetic leg and threw it at her with all the strength he had. The move caught her by surprise and almost knocked her over when the wooden leg hit her chest. The leg fell to the floor with a loud thump, and Anna rubbed her collarbone.

"This is all your fault! All of it. You should have left me to die in that prison camp," Stan growled at her.

"Don't say that," Anna said with a shaky voice as she picked up the prosthetic and set it on a nearby chair. "Don't you ever dare say that again."

"Why not? It's true. I'd rather be dead than a cripple. You did this to me."

Anna placed her hands on her hips, rising to her full height. "You ungrateful bastard!"

"Is everything alright in here?" a passing nurse asked.

Anna nodded and then walked over and closed the door, keeping her voice lowered when she spoke to him again. "You are the most ungrateful man I've ever encountered and I'm beginning to regret that I ever saved your life."

"You shouldn't have." Stan's flaring temper was already receding and he regretted being so violent. Even though self-righteousness clawed at every crevice inside him, he shouldn't have hit her with that damn leg.

"Peter would be ashamed, heartbroken even, he if knew that you're paying back his sacrifice by acting like a self-centered wimp who cares about nobody but himself." She took a step toward him, her eyes glaring daggers, and Stan involuntarily inched away from her. "Your brother gave up everything for you."

"You don't know that," Stan fired back to keep the guilt from trickling into his conscience.

"No, you're right. I don't know whether he's dead or

alive. But I know that he's being marched from one camp to another for hundreds of miles through snow and ice. And I know that a huge percentage of prisoners who start out will die along the way. Do you think Peter will be in the minority who survives?"

Stan paused and shook his head. "I didn't know that he'd been transferred."

"He's been transferred twice. The first time by rail car. The second one is still ongoing. Five hundred miles. That's the distance from Gross Born in Pomerania to Sandbostel where they are headed. On foot. It's been six weeks and no one knows exactly where they are or if they will ever return. The officials are merely counting the number of dead bodies left along the side of the road."

"Anna...I'm sorry." The rage fell off him like dirt under the shower, leaving a surge of shame in its wake. Shame over being so selfish. Peter had possibly sacrificed his life for him and what had he done?

"Don't be sorry. Be a man. Start by learning to walk." With treacherously damp eyes she pressed the wooden leg into his arms and left the room.

Stan stared at the door closing behind Anna's back. He'd promised his brother to take care of Anna and Jan until Peter returned. And that's exactly what he would do, because Stanislaw Zdanek never backed down from a promise.

He'd been selfish and allowed himself to wallow in self-pity for much too long. The truth of Anna's recriminations finally settled in, bone deep. He had to accept this new version of reality. He cautiously eyed the wooden leg on his lap. Could that...thing...really help him learn to walk again?

Maybe he wasn't doomed to spend his life as a useless member of society begging for charity?

Stan vowed to make an effort at least. He'd ask the young blonde nurse – not Anna because he didn't want to admit his change of mind to her just yet – to teach him how to put on the leg and what to do next.

CHAPTER 29: PETER

The bleak march progressed and on the day of the spring equinox Peter collapsed onto a bunk at the prisoner camp in Sandbostel, less than seventy miles away from Fallingbostel where he'd started his murderous trip two and a half months ago.

The long winter march had taken everything out of him and he had no idea how he'd managed to survive when so many had died. Throughout the past two weeks the weather had warmed. Bright green leaves budded on the trees and flowers poked their heads through the ground, announcing the arrival of spring. Normally, the renewal of spring would bring a smile to Peter's face, but sick, hungry and tired as he was, he cared for nothing but sleep and food.

The deep gnawing pain of hunger torturing him every minute of every day had become his constant companion, squeezing the smallest joy out of life. He'd never known that hunger – real, raw, unabated hunger – could be worse than any other pain.

A kind soul had distributed one slice of bread to each of the newcomers as they staggered into the camp, in rows of five, holding each other up because none of them could walk on their own.

Peter closed his eyes, the ferocious pain in his stomach appeased for a while with the slice of bread, reveling in the softness of the bed. For the first time in two months he didn't sleep on concrete or ice. To him, the wooden bunk with a worn-out blanket as mattress felt like the canopy bed of a princess. His tortured bones protruding against the skin welcomed the unfamiliar softness and he fell asleep the moment his head hit the blanket.

During the murderous march his emotions had started out with fear, then turned to renewed hatred for the Nazis when they'd executed Bartosz in cold blood. But soon the hatred had given way to remorse for not having snatched the chance at freedom when Anna had offered it. Remorse was followed by guilt – guilt to be alive when so many others weren't.

But now, collapsed onto the comparative comfort of a bunk under a roof, he didn't have any emotions left, but apathy. He couldn't care less about what would happen next. He didn't care whether he died today or tomorrow or not at all. What difference did it make in the grand scheme of such awful, cruel suffering?

He just...was. Dangling from the hands of his cruel puppeteers, dancing to their tune on strings of listlessness. The Nazis had finally reached their goal and reduced him to a non-human. An animal that merely existed with no thoughts of its own.

Peter woke from his own coughs and pressed his hands

against his ribs to ease the pangs of pain caused by his coughing. Even half asleep his feet set into motion with a mind of their own, thinking they were still on the endless march. But something felt different. Softer. He groaned as he rolled across his raw spine, opening his eyes into small slits.

Memories of the day before rushed back to assault him. Just when he thought he couldn't walk another step, they'd been shoved past the barbwire fence that surrounded his new home. He would never have believed he'd reach the point where he considered being held in an overcrowded, disease-infested prison camp a good thing. But he couldn't have been happier to see a prison camp from the inside.

No more walking.

"Get up! Roll call!" a voice bellowed and Peter hurried to get his meager bones off the bunk and into the assembly yard. Orders were given, prisoners assigned to work parties, corpses hauled away.

He settled into camp life, miserable but predictable. Definitely an improvement over marching through ice and snow. The weather warmed by the day, finally returning the warmth to his bones that had been absent for so many months. Even the mud that caked shoes and clothes was finally drying up, and with the sunshine, his cough began to improve.

After a few days Peter began to believe he might survive this war after all. Allied aircraft roamed the sky like they owned it, which was probably true, because he rarely ever saw the Luftwaffe defending their airspace.

Germany was truly on her knees, one last feeble attempt to rear up against the overwhelming strength of her enemies, before the inevitable happened and the awful six-year-long war would finally be over.

The prisoners were starved for news, as the guards had become increasingly tight-lipped about the progress at the front line. That probably was a good sign, although Peter and his comrades itched to know just how good. How near were the Allies? How soon would they be liberated? How much longer did they have to hang on to the thin thread of their lives?

Only three weeks later, as Peter's sore and injured feet had just healed, all the officers were set on the march again. Peter envied the majority who were allowed to stay, even with a typhus epidemic holding the camp in its deathly grip.

Anything but walking again.

So he walked.

Northeast.

One hundred miles. More or less retracing his tortured steps from whence he'd come.

Again.

The area seemed familiar. They passed around Hamburg in the North and Peter rubbed his eyes as he observed the previously proud and beautiful city reduced to a picture of apocalyptic devastation. His heart grew weary thinking of Anna and Jan. Were they still alive?

At least the weather had changed and he now longer had to brave wind and ice. But the sunshine brought out the bugs, the lice and the mosquitoes, feasting on the blood of the prisoners who were too weak to fend them off.

After two days marching from sunrise to sunset in the spring sun, his eyes were sore and weeping from the burn, his head about to explode from the exposure to the sun, and his face blistered with sunburn.

He kept walking. He dreamt about walking to the end of the world and tumbling down. His legs moved even when he lay on the ground trying to sleep. He thought he'd never stop walking again.

Evil truly knew no bounds and conditions were never so bad that they couldn't get worse..

A week later they arrived at their destination – Lübeck – and Peter wondered how many more times he'd be forced to crisscross Germany on foot, fleeing from the Russians in the East or the Western Allies in the West.

At the Oflag X-C they were crammed into already crowded barracks. As exhaustion overtook him, Peter made his way to a corner and crumpled to the ground. One of the existing prisoners shoved a stale piece of bread into his hands, and Peter simply looked at it.

He knew he needed to eat, but the effort required to raise his arm was too much to bear. The other prisoner seemed to notice, removed the bread from his hand again and broke off a small piece, forcing it into Peter's mouth.

Peter chewed automatically, far beyond feeling embarrassed for having to be fed like a baby. The other man held a cup of water to his lips and Peter greedily drank before coughing wracked his thin frame. Then he closed his eyes, his head leaning against the wall as sleep overtook him.

Despite the kindness of the other man, who'd probably saved his life, Peter couldn't find a sliver of hope in this place.

Only bleakness.

One week passed and Peter slowly returned from the

nearly-dead. His apathy slipped away and with every rumor rampaging through the camp he got up his hopes and his determination to live just a little more.

A second week passed and on May 2nd the miracle happened.

"British soldiers!" someone yelled at the top of his lungs.

CHAPTER 30: STAN

April 1945 in Berlin

Stan had been transferred to the prison hospital and despite being depressed and surly he made an effort to practice walking with the wooden leg. After a while he got the hang of it and he finally saw light at the end of the tunnel.

He'd prove to the world that even with only one leg he was still a valuable member of society. A real man.

Taking a deep breath, Stan pushed away from the wall and forced himself to focus on just one thing: walking. The distance between the two opposite walls of the room looked huge. Terrifying. Insurmountable.

The first steps went fine, but then he staggered putting weight on the prosthetic. Swaying like a flag in the wind he raised his arms to recapture his balance, to no avail. The floor came rushing up and he flattened his face on the hard linoleum. The sharp odor of cleansing agent tickled his nose and he sneezed.

Frustrated, Stan rolled over and pushed himself into a sitting position, before he used his hands and his good leg to move to the bed and heave himself up again. One hand secured to the bed frame, he hobbled back to the wall.

Starting over.

It took countless attempts until he reached the other side of the room without falling. Stan broke out into a huge grin, pumping his fist into the air, just to throw himself off balance again with the sudden movement. He bumped his behind into the wall for support and laughed out loud.

The door opened and a small person slid inside. Stan had never asked what kind of story Anna had spun to get a permit for Jan to visit him every day without fail. Perhaps nobody cared either way and the nurses were glad for every little bit of help they got tending to the prisoners.

"Hello, Jan, wanna see this? I think I finally got the hang of it."

Jan watched with eyes wide as saucers as Stan walked the entire distance with only a minor wobble.

"Fabulous, Uncle Stan! You're fabulous!" Jan rushed over to wrap his arms around Stan and if it weren't for the steady support of the windowsill, they'd both have tumbled to the floor.

"Hold your horses!" Stan chuckled.

"You're laughing…" Jan said, shaking his head in disbelief.

"What's so…" …*strange about it?* Stan wanted to ask, but stopped mid-sentence, guilt over his self-loathing selfishness making him frown. "I'm sorry. From now on I'll laugh more often, agreed?"

"Promise?"

"Promise!" They knocked fists to seal the deal.

With Jan's help he managed to walk the whole length of the hallway without falling, but by that time, his stump was swollen and burning from the heavy exercise. As soon as he settled on his bed, he noticed the boy's stony face.

"What's wrong? Something happened at home?" he asked, once again feeling the guilt for his own selfishness. Jan's face expressed his distress, and Stan hadn't given a single thought to the boy for the past hour.

"Anna and Grandma are so tense, but they won't tell me what's wrong. They whisper and look afraid, but put on fake smiles when I come into the room. Do you think they are angry at me?" Jan's eyes welled up with tears. Despite having to take on the responsibilities of an adult, he still was a child and it tore at Stan's heart to see him so sad.

"I'm sure they aren't angry at you." Stan had a pretty good idea what Anna and her mother were worried about and it certainly had nothing to do with Jan.

"But what else could it be?"

Stan had to smile. "The war? The Red Army has been shelling Berlin for days without pause and it's only a matter of time until the war is over."

"But that's a good thing, isn't it?"

"Yes. Now go home, and don't get caught in skirmishes." Stan patted Jan's shoulder and held in his thoughts. The end of the war wouldn't be a good thing for everyone, and Anna and her mother had every reason to be afraid.

He'd seen firsthand what happened when the Red Army

liberated a town. Vomit rose in his throat as he remembered the crimes against humanity he'd witnessed during his time as a forced conscript in the Red Army. Ruthless. Dedicated.

His own nation Poland had suffered – and continued to suffer – so direly under both occupiers. Between the Nazis and the Soviets, there really was no better choice.

For the Berlin females, though, being exposed to the capriciousness of a Soviet soldier would prove to be a thousand times worse than Hitler's cronies. Any woman who was merely raped and then left alone could consider herself lucky. Hundreds of thousands of women across Eastern Europe would testify to this.

Stan hated the Nazis with every fiber of his soul, but no woman, Nazi or not, deserved to be treated in such a way. Well, maybe with the exception of Irma Grese, the sadistic guard in Auschwitz half the Home Army whispered about with repugnance.

More bile rose in his throat and he screamed with frustration, as he realized that even after his liberation, he wouldn't be in a position to protect the women in his family. With only one leg to rely on, he needed a better plan.

In the following days the Battle for Berlin intensified. Stan could hear the constant shelling, artillery fire, gunfire, yelling and screaming. The nurses told him about man-to-man fighting in the debris-ridden streets of Berlin.

One morning a troop of Russian soldiers stormed the prison hospital, chasing the nurses and doctors away and freeing Stan. But where should he go?

Thankfully, Jan ventured into the hospital later in the day during one of his increasingly infrequent visits. Confused at the lack of guards or medical staff he asked, "What happened here?"

"The Soviets freed us, and then left to fight somewhere else."

"So why are you still here?"

Stan rubbed his chin, half amused and half dumbfounded at Jan's naivety. "Because I have nowhere else to go." *And I don't dare venture on my own through the streets crawling across rubble and getting caught up in a skirmish.*

With one leg.

The boy tilted his head, saying, "You will come with me, Uncle Stan."

"I can't possibly impose…" Stan shrunk from the idea of having to beg Anna's mother to host him.

"Off course you can, since you're family. Now, come." Jan held out his hand and Stan shrugged. It wasn't like he had much of a choice. At the end of the hallway he peeked into the deserted nurse's office. The Russians had raided it for everything of value, but miraculously the closet with bandage materials seemed intact. Stan had an idea.

"We don't want to return empty-handed. Come and help me." He opened the closed door and directed Jan to crouch down and rifle through the compartments at the bottom while he did the same at the top. They stuffed bandages and the meager remains of medicine into their pockets, and it didn't take long for Stan to find what he was looking for.

He let out a low whistle. "Here you are, sweethearts." With a grin he slid two bottles of pure alcohol for disinfection into the pockets of his jacket.

"What's this?" Jan asked, holding up a glass bottle with a transparent liquid.

Stan opened it and sniffed. The strong, stinging smell on an empty stomach overwhelmed his senses for a moment. When the dizziness stopped, he took a good gulp and reveled in the slow burn all the way into his stomach. "*Korn*," he answered. "It's the German equivalent to vodka and this one is good stuff. Put it in your satchel."

They left the nurse's office, ready to take on the world. But they got only as far as the stairs.

"Holy shit!" Stan had forgotten he was on the second floor of this building and that to get out he had to brave these damn stairs. His prosthetic could bend at the knee, but Stan was still struggling to make it do exactly as he intended, and he'd never before tackled stairs.

"You can do this, Uncle Stan. I'll hold you up." Jan beamed with pride.

"If you say so." Stan seriously doubted Jan could be of much help. Despite his malnourished condition he easily weighed more than double the young boy. "But I think I'll try on my own first."

He held onto the stair railing for dear life as he somehow managed to wobble, hop and slide down the stairs, supporting himself with his arms and his good leg. After what seemed like an hour he took one last stair to step on flat ground, panting and gasping. Stan wiped the sweat from his forehead, taking a few minutes to calm his thundering heart after the superhuman effort he'd just exerted.

"Let's go," he said to Jan. "We want to be at Anna's place before dark."

"It's not far." Jan soothed his unspoken worries. "I can

get there in no time at all, but with you it might take a bit longer."

Jan led him through hidden alleys, dodging the areas of open street fighting and always hiding in the shadows of the few remaining buildings. Everything went considerably well, until they reached a pile of debris scattered across the street, almost waist-high.

"We can't go around, because there's a crater bigger than two tanks," Jan said, giving a shrug. "We have to clamber across."

"We what?" Stan thought he hadn't heard right. "What makes you think I can clamber?"

"Come on, you did the stairs just fine. See, I can go with one leg, too," Jan said and hopped onto the debris, jumping a few times with on leg high in the air, until he lost his balance and quickly used his other leg to steady himself.

"Careful. We don't want to break the bottle of *Korn*," Stan called out with a chuckle. With a Herculean effort he somehow managed to cross the pile of rubble, more by creeping than walking, but he arrived on the other side, proud of himself.

It took them close to three hours until they finally arrived at the badly shelled building where the Klausen family lived. Stan was bathed in sweat, his heart pumping like crazy and he collapsed onto the stairs the moment Jan opened the door.

Jan rushed off to see if Anna was home and minutes later she appeared in front of him with an incredulous yet admiring expression on her face. "You walked all the way here on your own?"

Despite being utterly exhausted he managed a chuckle. "Didn't think I'd make it, but Jan here forced me to."

"Well done. Both of you," she said. "Lean on me. I'll help you downstairs."

Downstairs? "I thought Jan said you lived in a two-bedroom apartment on the fourth floor?" He was secretly relieved he wouldn't have to tackle four flights of stairs.

"We used to," Anna said, nodding. "Bombing damaged the building and it wasn't safe to stay upstairs so I salvaged what I could and we moved into the basement." She shrugged. "All the renters from the upper floors did…"

Frau Klausen was sitting in the basement preparing food on a tiny gas stove. She looked up at the incoming persons and shrank back, her eyes wide and glassy like a deer caught in the headlights of a vehicle. Not that there were deer or vehicles in Berlin. Or even electric lights.

"He's a friend," Anna said, calming her mother's fear. "Mutter, this is Stan Zdanek, Peter's brother. I told you about him."

"Stan, this is my mother, Frau Klausen."

"Thank you, Frau Klausen," Stan said, feeling slightly out of place. "I don't mean to impose on you but since the hospital was liberated and with no place to go, my nephew insisted…"

"Herr Zdanek—"

"Stan, please."

"Stan, then." Frau Klausen paused for a moment to point at the basement room with only a small metal-grilled window near the ceiling. "This is all we have, but you're welcome to share it with us."

"Thank you, Frau Klausen." Stan followed the movement

of her hand with his eyes. Frau Klausen and Anna had done their best to make the cold, dark basement into a cozy place with mattresses, a small cupboard, suitcases for clothing, a kitchen table and three chairs.

"I can go upstairs and get another mattress and a chair for you," Anna offered.

"Didn't you say it was unsafe?"

She shrugged. "There's a huge hole in the kitchen wall and all the windows are broken, but I can still go in and out when I'm careful. We just can't live and sleep there anymore. Since we neither have electricity nor running water it's not much better in the apartment anyway than down here."

Stan nodded, although he didn't buy into her forced cheerfulness. A cold, musty basement was still a cold musty basement.

CHAPTER 31: ANNA

On May 2nd, 1945, Berlin surrendered to the Russians and the looting, raping and murdering started in earnest.

Worry infiltrated every cell in Anna's body. For three days they hadn't left the basement except for short trips to the well in the backyard to get fresh water. Usually, she went together with Jan so they'd be quicker. Straining her ears for any unfamiliar sound she'd pump the water at full speed while he switched out the containers under the stream of water. Then they'd haul the buckets for her family and the elderly lady living in the cellar compartment next to them back downstairs as fast as they could.

Her mother and Stan would always wait inside, and she'd see the secret relief washing over their faces when she and Jan returned. But Anna didn't delude herself into believing they were safe in that basement.

Just because the Russians hadn't arrived at their street yet didn't mean they wouldn't. Whenever frightening thoughts crept up, she forcefully pushed them away. It didn't make sense to cackle over unlaid eggs. If worst came to worst, then she'd worry about it. Not now.

"We're running out of food," Mutter said with a grave voice. "I'll go upstairs and see what we have left in the pantry."

"I took the last couple of potatoes yesterday. There's nothing left except for a quarter cup of salt," Anna answered. A silence fell over the small room. After a while she offered, "I'll go to the store and see if I can get anything."

"You can't. It's too dangerous. The Russian soldiers…" Stan said.

Anna knew all too well about the soldiers and their infamous command, *Komm, Frau.* Come with me, woman. It never led to anything good, but it also was an offer no German woman could refuse – usually backed up with the persuasiveness of a gun should the woman show any signs of disobedience.

"We can't stay without food for God knows how long. Someone has to go," Anna insisted, rubbing her temple.

"I'll do it," Stan said, rising from his chair.

"You? No way. You don't even know where the stores are."

"You could give me directions."

"Anna is right. You can't go. The grocery store owners don't know you. They won't give you a thing." Frau Klausen glanced up for a moment from her mending.

"I'll go then," Jan offered and Anna's head jerked around at the same time as those of the two other adults.

"It's not that I haven't done it before. I know the area.

The grocery ladies like me. I can run fast if needed. And I speak Russian—"

"You do?" Anna asked. Here was this twelve-year-old boy who spoke flawless German, English and Russian, in addition to his mother-tongue Polish, while she'd barely mastered some English.

"Where we come from, most of the people speak three or four languages," Stan explained.

"It's still too dangerous, he's only a child," Frau Klausen said with a stern voice.

"They don't go after boys," Anna said in a soft voice. She hated to send Jan outside to get food, but truth be told he was the most likely to succeed without getting hurt.

"Here, take your satchel and the ration cards." Frau Klausen got up to help Jan ready himself. She pressed a kiss on the top of his head. "Godspeed, my boy."

The three adults stayed in the cellar room, each one coping with the worry about Jan in a different way. Mutter mended clothes. Stan carved a spoon from a small branch. And Anna peeled potatoes.

Suddenly steps on the staircase and loud knocks at the rusty metal basement door jerked them up from their separate tasks. Anna jumped, ferocious angst grabbing her by the throat and making breathing difficult.

The knocking became angry and she knew they'd break the door in no time at all if she didn't open it. With one long gaze at her mother she took a deep breath and called out "C—"

But before the word could leave her mouth, a big hand pressed on her face and Stan said, "Shush. Let me."

She nodded, petrified, and the hand slipped away. Stan

limped to the door on his crutches and opened it. Anna strained her ears to hear, but she couldn't understand the angry shouting.

~

Stan's heart hammered against his ribs and he wished he'd bothered to strap on his prosthetic leg earlier today. But since he wasn't about to leave the basement, he hadn't seen the need.

He opened the door on crutches and stared into the dilated eyes of roused soldiers looking to have some fun. Judging by the boozy breath they'd already started the party.

"We...want...woman," they chanted in broken German.

Stan considered for a moment how best to address them and then decided to speak in their own language, "I'm sorry. There's just me."

The ringleader stepped forward and pushed Stan aside. "I'd rather see for myself."

A group of six soldiers trampled into the basement checking each of the empty compartments until they arrived at the end of the hallway. To the left was the elderly lady, well above eighty, and to the right were Anna and her mother.

The ringleader turned right. Moments later Stan heard Anna's high-pitched yelp across the noise of rowdy joking. He hurried as best as he could to the compartment, his hands clutched to the crutches.

"*Schöne Frau. Komm,*" one of the men said, yanking Anna toward him by a strand of her blonde hair. Her blouse and bodice were ripped open, exposing the white flesh of her breasts to the group of leering men. Another one yanked at the arms of Frau Klausen, who crouched huddled into a corner of the room.

"Please, leave them alone," Stan begged, hot rage boiling in his body.

"No chance. We came here to have fun. And this one," he pointed at Anna, "looks like plenty of fun."

Dizziness invaded Stan's brain. Never in his life before had he felt as helpless as he did now. He'd promised his brother to care for his family. Peter had sacrificed his chance at freedom, maybe even his very life, and how was Stan going to repay him? By watching Peter's wife and mother-in-law being gang-raped by a bunch of squiffy Soviet bastards.

He spied the knife Anna had used to peel potatoes lying on the floor and considered whether he could pick it up and cut the soldier's throat with it. It took less than a second to accept the futility of the attempt. Even if he still had both legs, he'd be shot before – or after – he killed the man, which wouldn't hinder the other five soldiers from raping the women.

"I want her first," the ringleader said, before he nodded at Stan with a dirty leer. "You can watch, cripple. Seeing a real man do your woman might even get you hard."

Logic and reason flew away and Stan surged forward, intent on strangling the despicable man. The Russian countered Stan's hapless attempt and shoved him backwards against the wall. Stan's head connected with the cold hardness of bricks and for a few moments stars circled in front of his eyes. In slow motion he slid to the floor, unable to regain his uprooted balance.

The ringleader looked down at him, his brows drawn together. "I do not like being disturbed." Then he nodded at the two youngest soldiers and said, "You watch him. Another move like this, cut off his other leg."

Rousing laughter followed the cruel words and the other men started clapping their hands and cheering their leader on as he loosened his belt. One of the young soldiers aimed his rifle at Stan, while the other one took great pleasure in producing a ten-inch knife and wielding it in front of Stan's face, before sliding it down his chest and slightly stabbing at his groin.

Stan closed his eyes, frozen with fear, shame and guilt. On a logical level he knew that his actions wouldn't change anything, but still, pain about his inactivity racked his heart.

An incomprehensible grunting followed a pained gasp. The men obstructed his view, but the sound of footfalls a few moments later indicated that the first perpetrator had finished and the remaining soldiers were now taking turns abusing the women.

Bile rose in Stan's throat and he balled his fists, swearing eternal revenge. He wished he could murder every single raping *Rotarmist* with his bare hands. He'd make them suffer; torture them slowly until they begged to be killed. And then he'd deny the wish with a smile.

When finally the men tucked themselves back into their uniforms, relief flooded Stan's system. But only for a moment, until he saw how the soldier currently watching him started tossing the knife back and forth from hand to hand, his expression twisted into a nasty sneer. "We could take a souvenir," the soldier slurred, his tongue thick with alcohol.

Stan's eyes widened as the meaning of the man's words and his gesture of cutting seeped into his brain. Adrenaline surged through his veins and with the strength of a truly desperate man he hauled himself up and yelled at the top of his lungs, "Wait!"

Six stupefied pairs of eyes stared at him.

"Wouldn't you rather have booze? I'll give it to you if you leave them unharmed."

The Russians' eyes lit up at the mention of booze. The leader took a step toward Stan and pushed his gun against Stan's chest. "What makes you think I can't have the booze and come back to finish them off?"

"Kill me and you'll never know where it is," Stan bluffed. The hidey-hole was easy enough to find even with a superficial search.

"Kill? I have better ways to make you talk."

"You had your fun. Take the booze and leave the women alive."

"They don't deserve to live." The soldier with the knife in his hands spit on the floor, the expression of hate in his eyes mixing with pain. "Even a slow and painful death is too good for these whores, after what the Nazi bastards did to my family."

Stan had a pretty good idea about the atrocities committed by the Nazis, and it hit him between the eyes: He wasn't one bit better than the six Russian soldiers standing in the room. Hadn't he just minutes ago sworn eternal revenge? Immeasurable suffering? The cruelest of pains? Another wave of shame hit him, this time for his own depreciable notions. Maybe it was time to try and break the vicious circle of violence?

He put on his most convincing expression as he jumped over his own shadow and extended a symbolic hand to the very people he hated so much. "Look. Comrade. I'm a Pole, I hate the Nazis as much as you do, and if the swine hadn't smashed my leg and captured me I'd be with you now taking dominion over Hitler's capital of Evil and punishing its citizens. But do you really want to mutilate these women because someone else committed an awful crime against your family? Wouldn't you rather enjoy the end of the war and live in peace?"

The other men paused their rowdy antics for a moment, staring in disbelief at Stan. Finally, one of them said, "Let's take the booze."

"We...want...booze," the rest began chanting and their leader nodded at Stan. "Show us and we'll leave you alone."

Stan nodded. "Follow me." He hobbled to the cubbyhole beneath the stairs and crouched down, afraid he'd never get up again. He handed the leader of the group the bottle of *Korn* he'd stolen from the hospital. The soldiers circulated the bottle, each one taking a long swallow, before the leader slid the bounty into his pocket. Stan awaited with bated breath what would happen next.

"Good stuff," the leader said and signaled his men to leave.

A heavy burden fell from Stan's shoulders as he heard the metal door clicking shut behind them. He was still crouched in the corner when Frau Klausen came around, extending her hand to help him up.

"Thank you," she said in her usual voice.

"I...I'm sorry. I..." Words failed him, the happenings still fresh in his mind.

"We don't talk about that. Ever," Frau Klausen said and handed him the sticks he'd used for crutches.

Anna had turned her back to the door of the compartment, arranging her clothes. Red-hot rage, followed by guilt shot through Stan's veins as he saw her slender back heaving with emotions.

He could only hope that the Soviet high command would impose discipline again and stop the repulsive behavior sooner rather than later. Or that the Americans arrived in Berlin.

About an hour later they heard another knock on the basement door. The tension in the room skyrocketed, Stan's neck hair standing on end. But a moment later he relaxed when the next knock carried the agreed-upon signal. Three quick knocks. Two long ones.

"It's Jan," Frau Klausen said, her voice thick with relief. "I'll go and open the door."

Stan used Frau Klausen's absence to ask the question that had been burning on his tongue, "Are you hurt?"

Anna shook her head. "No. Just shaken up. Thanks for your intervention." She swallowed hard.

"I...I'm sorry..."

"Don't." No doubt fighting against her tears, she stubbornly avoided his gaze, but he'd already seen the immeasurable agony in her face. And it was his fault. For failing to protect her. If only...it didn't help that he saw his brother's face in his mind and heard his last words, begging him to take care of his family. *Hell of a good caretaker I am!* A sarcastic smile pursed his lips, before another wave of guilt threatened to undo him.

A moment later, Jan rushed into the room shrieking, "Look what I got!"

"Let's see what you have," Anna said with a cheerful voice that sounded so fake, it rang in Stan's ears.

"Bread and carrots." He pulled two immense loaves of bread from his satchel and handed them over to Anna.

"The bakery gave you all of this?" Anna said with wide eyes.

Jan turned red and hung his head, mumbling, "Not really. I stole it."

Stan reached over and lifted the boy's head up. "You stole it?"

"I'm sorry, but the bakery windows were all broken up and everyone was taking what they could. These loaves of bread had fallen under the counter. I crawled underneath and grabbed them. No one saw me do it," he assured.

Stan shook his head. "There's nothing wrong with what you did. I'm sure the baker would be happy to know that the work of her hands was going to help feed hungry German mouths and not those of the Red Army."

"What about Polish mouths?" Jan asked hesitantly, bringing into the open what everyone had been denying for months.

"I think given the choice between the Red Army and a Pole, the baker would most certainly choose the Pole." Stan kept his tone light and tried to steer the conversation to lighter things. They ate the bread Jan had pilfered together with the few remaining potatoes and talked about happier times.

CHAPTER 32: PETER

Five days after his liberation he was still staying at the former prisoner camp, hastily converted into a hospital and Displaced Persons Camp. With fighting rampant all over the area, the British had ordered everyone to stay around.

The liberated prisoners were free to leave the camp, but not the town. Most used their new freedom to pilfer and loot anything they could get a hold of, since the new British commander had announced that the town of Lübeck was "a lawless zone with looting allowed" for the next three days. Hordes of ex-prisoners ventured out to take the much-needed food out of the Germans' hands. Civilians – mostly women – scurried away with terror-stricken faces as soon as they saw the shabby men coming into town.

Peter hated committing such blatant war crimes, and he was grateful for his weakened condition that allowed him the perfect excuse to stay in the hospital during the day.

"Major, when can I leave?" Peter asked the British military doctor.

"We have started to repatriate the British and American soldiers already, but there's still fighting going on in Poland so you'll have to stay at least until the war is over. Which can't be much longer."

"I don't want to return to Poland. I need to find someone first."

The doctor gave him a scrutinizing glance. "Where do you need to go?"

"Berlin."

"Berlin?" the doctor gasped. "That city is off limits. And from all I hear no civilian in their right mind should go there. The Soviets are out for revenge, murdering the men and raping the women."

Peter swallowed hard. "I...I have to go. My wife and my son are there. I'll go with a pass or without."

The doctor cast him a sympathetic look, but didn't ask further questions. "As soon as Germany has capitulated, I'll clear you to leave the British zone for Poland. What you do on your way is out of my hands."

"Thanks, Major."

At least Peter could hold onto this sliver of hope. Sick with worry for Anna and Jan, he consoled himself with the fact that Stan was with them and would do anything to protect them.

He had crisscrossed this damn country so many times already in the last few months, what difference would walking another two hundred miles through battlefields make? But he knew well that, in his debilitated physical condition, he'd never make it. And he didn't want to run into the Red Army without a valid pass. Getting shipped to a Siberian Gulag was the last thing he needed.

Later in the afternoon, a commotion outside caught his attention. A group of ex-prisoners dragged several guards with bound wrists and ankles behind them.

"Hang 'em! Hang 'em!" chanted the crowd.

Peter rushed outside to try and prevent the worst. The guards probably deserved their punishment, but Peter still thought a mob lynching would put them at the same level with the Nazis. They were better than that.

Courts would rule and let justice prevail, not vigilantism. But when he reached the courtyard, he skidded to a halt. Four men dangled from lampposts in the soft breeze. Peter gagged. Would the horrors never end?

Would the victors now do unto the Germans as the Germans had done unto them? An eye for an eye. A tooth for a tooth. He bit on his lip, scared with the prospect of a violent and bleak future in Europe. He sank to his knees, knowing that he must go to Berlin if he wanted to find Anna and Jan alive.

The next morning, on May 8th, the men woke to the good news of Germany's unconditional surrender. Peter gave a scream of joy. The war was over. And he had survived.

In the late morning the doctor came and gave him clearance to leave the hospital, handing him a travel pass to Poland. "Good luck. You'll need it."

Peter caught a ride on the back of a truck filled with replacement parts for machinery. During his death march across Germany he'd been too exhausted to raise his eyes from the ground in front of his feet, but now from up on the truck's bed he became aware of the utter devastation marring the formerly beautiful country. Thousands upon thousands of displaced persons roamed the streets, everyone trying to get home, or to find surviving family members.

Former POWs, concentration camp survivors, refugees from the East, and German civilians seemed to be everywhere. They scattered like leaves on the sea, sloshing with the tide. Up and down. Left and right. Nothing but scorched earth. Cities and towns in ruins. Uncultivated fields.

Being raised on a farm, he knew that those who hadn't sowed in spring wouldn't harvest in fall. It would be a dreadful winter with little food for the already starving population.

But at least the weapons had been laid to rest.

Several days later, after changing his means of transportation countless times, he finally reached the outskirts of Berlin. He hardly believed his eyes. The trip from Lübeck had given him a good view of the devastation, but Berlin surpassed his wildest nightmares.

A city in ruins – almost no house remained intact. Corpses littered the streets, and the people who braved the chaos on the rubble-strewn streets and ventured outside resembled zombies. With bated breath he first went to the employee housing at the Charité where he and Anna had both lived before he left for Warsaw almost a year ago.

Both buildings had been razed to the ground. By some

miracle the hospital building still stood, but upon inquiry he found out that the Russians had taken over the care of the patients and sent all the nurses home.

Just where was Anna's home now? Without a better idea he walked – relatively unchallenged in his Polish uniform – to the place where Anna's mother lived. When he arrived in front of the building, he took a deep breath. Where the apartment had been was only a gaping hole in the wall. But since the building itself seemed to hold up well enough, he ventured inside.

A boy scurried past him, trying to escape into the basement, but Peter held out his arm and grabbed the boy's shoulder. Pushing, shoving, kicking and biting, the boy tried to free himself from Peter's grip.

"Wait, I just want to ask a question."

"That's what they all say," the boy answered, kicking Peter painfully in the shin.

"Ouch!" Peter yelped and let go of the boy, who turned around, his glacial blue eyes filling with disbelief.

A moment later, he flung himself into Peter's arms, almost toppling both of them over. "Dad! You're back!"

"Janusz. My son. My dearest Jan." Peter was moved to tears, pressing his eyes tightly shut so as not to give away his powerful emotions. "You're alive. Is…Anna?"

"Come with me," Jan said with the brightest smile, and a multitude of stones tumbled from Peter's chest.

Anna must have heard them coming, because she appeared in the hallway. She took his very breath away, still the most beautiful woman on earth, despite the fact that her hair was unkempt and she'd smeared dirt across her face.

Her clothes were dusty, torn, and bagging on her tiny frame. Her beautiful eyes still shone with the steel will to survive, although the light in them had dimmed.

"Anna, sweetheart. My baby. My love." Peter hugged her tight and could feel the suppressed sobs racking her body.

"You survived," she stated matter-of-factly, as she leaned against his bony chest. Gone was the exuberant women who'd rushed into his arms in Fallingbostel. Something was amiss, but Peter didn't know what. Although he feared for the worst.

Jan grabbed his hand. "Uncle Stan and Grandma will be so happy to see you."

"So Stan made it," Peter murmured to Anna.

She responded with a small smile. "But just barely."

"Like all of us," Peter said.

"There's something you should know. He's..." Anna started to say, but Jan was already pulling him forward to the small cellar compartment.

Peter staggered backwards the moment he saw Stan huddling on the floor with only one leg. But he did his best not to show his shock and walked over to give his brother a big hug. "Man, I thought I'd never see you again."

"Very nearly you didn't."

"Good to see you back." Frau Klausen's voice came from behind and Peter turned around to greet her. Anna's mother had aged considerably in the past year, and she truly looked like an old and broken woman now.

"Thank you, Frau Klausen. I hope I'm not too much of a burden."

She shook her head. "We don't have much."

"That's alright. I'll start looking for work this very afternoon."

"You could start with reconstructing the wall in the apartment, then we can move back up there," Jan suggested.

Peter chuckled. He was quite handy, but he feared his son had too much trust in his abilities as a mason.

CHAPTER 33: ANNA

Peter was starting to grow weary of her minimal answers and lack of enthusiasm. But every he touched her, her skin crawled under the force of the awful memories. Stan had never told her, but she was pretty sure, he'd prevented worse when he'd bribed them with booze. And while she was truly grateful, sometimes she wished he'd let them kill her. At least then she wouldn't have to endure the images in her head. Nor the feel of groping hands on her naked skin. The smell of alcohol on their lips. Repulsed at the memory, she gagged.

"Are you sure, you're alright?" Peter asked for the umpteenth time, so much sorrow in his eyes. She really should be better at hiding her distress from him. With everything he'd been through he didn't need a wife who flinched every time he touched her.

Thankfully, they slept in the crowded compartment with five persons including a child, so he never tried to become intimate with her, but she knew that only bought her some time. One day, she had to attend to her marital duties again. Another shudder racked her slim body as earlier memories bubbled up that she'd carefully locked deep inside.

"I'll go into the backyard to wash our clothes," Anna said. They still had no running water in the building, but the garden well still pumped up fresh and clean water.

"Let me help you with the pump," Peter said and cast Stan a glance. Stan in return engaged Jan in conversation.

"That's really not necessary," she said, goosebumps sneaking up her spine. This was a ploy to catch her alone. Best to play innocent and ignore whatever Peter had in mind.

"It is."

"Well then, let's go." She pushed the bundle with their spare clothing into his arms, while she grabbed a bucket and a piece of soap.

Peter pumped water into the bucket and she got busy wetting down the clothes and applying soap to them. Peter helped her and she started to relax, thinking that he might let her behavior go for now.

She was wrong.

"Anna, tell me what happened," Peter asked after a while.

She shook her head, "Not much. We pretty much hid in the basement while there was fighting in the streets..."

"Anna, I know you too well to believe this crap. You think I haven't noticed? The way you flinch away whenever I touch you?"

She knew that stubborn expression on Peter's face and sighed. He wasn't about to let her pretend nothing was wrong. Anna closed her eyes and cleared her throat. "It was bad. I've never been more afraid..." She grabbed one of Jan's shirts and began rinsing the soap from the fabric. The mundane routine was her lifeline for sanity. "…I couldn't understand what they were saying, but the intent was clear. I felt so helpless. So…Stan tried to help me, but there were six of them. Two of them held him at gunpoint while the others took turns…I…my mother…I was sure they'd kill both of us. You hear so many awful things…I mean, they are the victors; they can do with us as they wish and nobody will even complain. "

Peter took the shirt from her hands and forced her to look at him. "Darling, I wish I'd been here to protect you. I'm so sorry…I should have left with you that day…"

For the first time it occurred to her that Peter blamed himself for what had happened to her and her reaction had only aggravated his guilt. Her eyes watered with compassion. She'd wanted to hide her suffering, to not heap more sorrow on him, and she'd actually made everything worse. She took the shirt back and continued squeezing the water from it.

"I thought they'd for sure cut my throat or mutilate me. I kept imagining Jan returning to the basement and finding our bodies lying there." She sniffed. "Stan must have thought the same, because he offered them alcohol if they'll let us live. And while I'll always be grateful, every time I see him I remember what happened."

A shudder racked her body and Peter came over to wrap his arms around her. She relaxed – just a little – into his embrace and continued scrubbing the clothes. "I try to tell myself that I've been raped before and survived, but this time…Doctor Tretter was a monster but at least I knew he wouldn't kill me."

"My poor darling. I wish I could make it all undone," he said with so much sorrow in his voice that tears sprang into her eyes. She wasn't the only one suffering. Each survivor had seen and experienced more than any person should have to.

While they were physically intact, mentally, they were both as crippled as Stan. And they could only hope that with time, patience and mutual love they'd one day leave all this behind and be happy again.

She leaned against Peter, thankful for his silence, and with every breath she relaxed a bit more into his embrace, the grief, anger, and fear slowly seeping from her bones. It would take a long time, but with Peter by her side, she'd one day be able to feel whole again.

CHAPTER 34: STAN

Time passed and Stan grew increasingly unhappy with his situation. The Western Allies had finally arrived in Berlin and divided the city into four sectors. The sector where he lived with the Klausen family was now under American control, which was a relief.

The Amis, as the Germans called them, were far from perfect, but a huge improvement compared to the Russians before. At long last the women could go outside again to get food without having to fear for their modesty.

Anna had returned to work as a nurse for the Americans. Stan meanwhile walked almost without a limp on his wooden leg and even stairs didn't pose a problem anymore. Which was good, because he and Peter had taken to reconstructing the outer wall of the Klausen apartment. And a few days ago they'd moved back onto the fourth floor.

But Stan didn't want to live on the charity of his married family anymore and grew more discontent every day.

"What's wrong with you, grumpy man?" Peter teased

him as they were fixing the splintered cupboards in the kitchen.

Stan merely sent him a dark stare and continued to carve out a piece of wood to use as a leg for the cupboard.

"From where I'm sitting, it seems you're intent on wallowing in self-pity." Peter kept pressing the issue.

Stan groaned. Off course, Peter had to play the caring-older-brother card now and pester him with good advice about life. When Peter was in that mood, there was nothing one could do, except shut up and listen.

"Are you still moping about your leg? You have managed so well, strangers don't even notice."

"You mean they don't gawk at me in pity?" Stan growled. He definitely wasn't in the mood for a lecture about the virtues in life.

"Just saying...here, help me and hold the waste pipe tight, while I..." With a clanking sound Peter yanked the pipe open and grimaced. "No wonder it won't work. You could build an entire house with the debris in here."

Stan continued carving and hoped his brother would forget about their earlier topic.

"If it's not the leg, what then?" Peter asked after a while.

"Dammit! Why do you have to stick your nose into my business?" Stan burst out.

"Because I'm your brother and I..."

"Stop the older brother bullshit and leave me in peace!"

"I'd do that, but you're not peaceful." They stared at each other and Stan felt a rush of adrenaline course through his veins, ready to pounce at his brother and settle the dispute with a good old-fashioned brawl.

Damn leg! I can't even have a fight with my brother!

He slumped against the wall and closed his eyes for a moment. "Know what? You're right. I'm not at peace. I'm a worthless piece of shit. I failed you. I failed her." Stan glared at his brother.

Peter stayed silent for a while, putting the pipe in place again and wiping his hands off. Then he turned around and said, "Oh, now we're getting somewhere. You're blaming yourself for what happened to Anna and her mother."

"Rightly so." Stan returned Peter's unnerving stare. Why wouldn't his brother understand that it was Stan's fault? Had Peter been in the basement he wouldn't have let those bastards have their way with Anna. "I'm worthless without my leg. I'm not even a real man anymore."

"Well, that may be your perspective, but from where I'm sitting you look like a real man to me, albeit one intent on wallowing in self-pity."

"You don't get it, do you?" Stan hissed with barely concealed anger. "Every time I look at Anna or her mother I see those Russians and my worthless self."

"Stan, let me ask you a question," Peter turned to face him. "What could you have done? With two legs, or even with a pistol? One man against six?"

The futility of his argument took the wind from his sails and Stan shook his head, "Nothing. But that doesn't make a difference. I should at least have tried."

"No, you shouldn't. Anna told me you probably saved her life."

Every single hair on Stan's body stood on end as he was transported back in time, seeing the gleaming blade in the soldier's hands.

Peter's big hand fell down on Stan's shoulder, squeezing

tight. "You may not believe me right now, but I'll be forever indebted to you. Without you Anna and her mother would both be dead or at least marked for life."

Stan sighed. The guilt weighed heavily on his conscience, despite logic and reason. Peter could talk all he wanted, but Stan would never fully forgive himself. "I hate being here! I hate not taking care of myself and being a burden to the Klausens. I hate the Germans. And I hate Berlin. I'm fed up with all this shit and I want ..." He stopped as it hit him right in the center of the chest what he needed to do. "I'll go home."

"You what?"

"You heard me right, I'll go home. To the farm."

"That's not a good idea. Not right now."

"Why not?" Stan asked.

"Because of the Soviets. They're still arresting Home Army and sending them to Siberia."

"You think they'd arrest a cripple like me? I'm not a threat to them. And I won't be of use in their Gulags either, so why bother?"

"Well, you might have a point there," Peter said, pursing his lips. "But traveling is cumbersome. Who'd go with you?"

"We could all go," Stan stubbornly said, although he knew full well that was wishful thinking.

"You know that's not possible." One couldn't simply travel across sections and borders without a permit and Anna would never get one for Poland. All Germans were being expelled from their former homelands in the East; they wouldn't welcome her in.

"Then I'll go alone. This is my last word on the subject." With his mind made up, he felt a wave of relief wash over him. He even cast a smile at his brother, happy about the future that waited for him.

"When?" Peter asked, eyeing him carefully.

"First thing in the morning. As much as I hate leaving you and Jan, this is something I have to do."

"Good luck. I'll accompany you to the train station," Peter offered.

"Just like that?" Stan tilted his head, eyeing his brother suspiciously. This sudden change of mind unsettled him.

Peter nodded and then clasped him in a tight hug. "I understand. I wouldn't stay in Berlin if it weren't for Anna. I'd probably try my luck in England."

Several days later Stan arrived at the family farm near Lodz. Or what was left of it. As he rounded the bend, he felt his heart break at the devastation that greeted him. More than a year ago SS brutes had torched the farm. The sooty stone walls stood intact, but the roof and all the furniture had been burnt. For now he'd have to live in the garden shed, which miraculously had survived the destruction.

He eyed the remains of his former home, a feeling of loneliness seeping deep into his bones. It would be a long, long time until the farm could be called a home again. He found jars with pickled vegetables, canned meat and a bottle of vodka in the secret pantry beneath the kitchen.

Since it was a warm summer evening, he settled outside, eating some of the food and downing the entire bottle of vodka throughout the night. Then he wept. Wept for the years of war, his abused and betrayed nation, the millions who died. He wept for his lost youth, the many lives he'd taken in battle, the many friends who'd died.

Finally he cried for the loss of his leg, his twin brother and his home.

The next morning he woke from the sound of a barking dog, his head ready to explode. He opened his eyes to tiny slits and closed them right away, because the bright sunshine multiplied his headache.

"Hey, you! Take a hike!" a shrill voice yelled at him.

Stan had no choice but to open his eyes to slits again. The barking dog stood a few feet away and a tall boy bent over him.

"Get off this ground. Or I'll tell the dog to chase you away." The yelling boy looked strangely familiar and slowly recognition trickled into Stan's foggy brain.

"Tadzio. It's me. Stan," he said in a hoarse voice. Damn alcohol.

"Stan?" Tadzio, the neighbor's boy, slowly approached him. "Is it really you? Why are you sleeping on the porch?"

Because I was too drunk and nostalgic to get up last night. "Help me up," he said, extending his hand to Tadzio. The boy, who must be thirteen by now, was amazingly strong and pulled Stan up without difficulty, only to stare in shock at Stan's trousers, where the wooden leg hung at a strange angle. "Doesn't that hurt?"

"Not anymore." Stan scoffed. "It's a prosthetic. The Germans kept my leg over there."

Tadzio's eyes widened, while Stan hopped to the wall and leaned against it pushing the prosthetic into the correct place.

"How's your mother?"

The boy kept staring at him, until he finally mumbled, "Fine. My little sister, too. And Rex, our new dog. Sorry for yelling at you, but there's so many vagrants passing and stealing everything that's not nailed down." A shadow of guilt crossed Tadzio's face. "We...we've been using your vegetable gardens and..."

Stan put an arm on Tadzio's shoulder. "And you can continue to do so. Thanks for taking care of the farm."

"Well, not really care. It's a shame what the SS swine did, but Mother and I have scared off everyone trying to occupy the farm. We knew you or your sister would come back one day."

"Do you know where Katrina is?" Stan asked.

"No. Last thing we heard was they had to flee from Bartosz's farm. It was in the middle of the battle lines for weeks. Bartosz's mom was killed."

Stan had met the nice woman a few times, but at the news of her death he shamefully felt relief. Now he wouldn't have to tell her that the last remaining of her four sons had been killed on one of the infamous death marches.

In the afternoon Tadzio's mother offered him a ride into town on a cow-drawn carriage, where he visited the Red Cross station and filed missing persons reports on his sister Katrina, his Jewish sister-in-law Agnieska and a couple of old friends. He also registered with the Russian administration, biting his tongue at the sharp remarks he wanted to say.

Back at the farm, he decided to mold his own future and began, with the help of neighbors, to repair the house and prepare the fields for cultivation. It was slow and tedious work, but every day he managed to do a little bit more.

With every effort at improvement, he still anticipated that one day soon, some of his displaced family and friends would show up at the farm. Every morning he awoke full of hope and every night, despair and grief crept into his heart. Maybe he should have stayed with Peter and Anna in Berlin?

CHAPTER 35: STAN

He had adapted into his new routine as a farmer. Getting up early, working all day, sleeping plagued with nightmares at night. With Tadzio's help, he'd cleared a small field, sowed wheat and planted potatoes. It was already late in the year to do so, but he hoped the weather would stay warm long enough to harvest in the fall.

The most urgent work done, he took on the Herculean task of removing the weeds and pronging the big field that extended behind the farmhouse all the way up to the forest. At noon, he settled in the shadow of a huge tree, fleeing from the scorching summer heat. He drank fresh water from his thermos and ate the vegetable soup Tadzio's mother had made.

He must have dozed off for a while, because when he opened his eyes again, he saw a woman traipsing through the vegetable garden near the house. Her shoulders were hunched forward and the formerly colorful dress she wore had faded into different hues of bluish-grey.

She looked lost. Desolate. One of the displaced persons who roamed the country looking for lost family members or a place to stay. She'd leave soon enough, or Tadzio's dog would chase her away. At second glance, her skinny frame tugged at his heartstrings.

"Dammit!" He used the tree to push himself up and walked the distance back to the house, seeing if he could help her along.

"Stan," the woman shouted at him. "Stan! You're here!" She rushed toward him and before he knew what was happening she fell into his arms.

"Agnieska? Is that you?"

She peeked up at him from under her heavy eyelashes and a cute blush crept across her face, as she peeled herself from his arms and smoothed down the faded dress. "I'm sorry. But...I had given up hope of finding anyone alive."

"Don't be sorry. It's good to see you." He pulled her into his arms again, enjoying the way her soft body felt in his arms. Sensations he'd thought didn't exist anymore flooded his system and pooled deep down in his groin.

"You must be hungry." Both of them chuckled at his words.

"Your mother, God bless her, used to say that all the time." Agnieska smiled at him, the smile converting her dusty, tired face into pure sunshine.

"I learned how to take care of myself and the farm. And food is what we all need most after six years of starving. Sit down." He motioned for her to sit on the porch at the rickety table that he'd scrounged just a week ago. "Tadzio's mother has made soup, I'll heat it up for you."

Agnieska nodded and fell into one of the two chairs. She

looked exhausted. And sad. And adorable. Stan disappeared into the kitchen and heated the soup for her. Just two days prior he'd finally managed to repair the stove.

"Here you go," he said, handing her the bowl and a slice of bread. Then he sat across the table and watched how she hungrily wolfed down her meal. She was awfully skinny, her arms frail. He told her the short version of his ordeals during the war, leaving out the part about his leg.

"Thank God, Janusz is safe. I was so worried about him," she mumbled, chewing her bread.

After a while he asked her, "Where have you been?"

The brilliance in her eyes dimmed and she cast them downward before she said, "After the Uprising the Nazis took me to Dresden to work in one of their ammunition factories. I thought I'd never make it...the bombing...so many of my coworkers were burnt alive..."

She shuddered in the bright sunshine and Stan hurried to say, "You don't have to tell me if it's too difficult."

Agnieska cast him a grateful smile, and blinked away a few tears. "I'm here now. The Russians liberated Dresden and I was lucky not to be a German woman." Her pale face turned even paler. "I came into a displaced persons camp and then made my way back to Warsaw, where I placed missing persons reports with the Red Cross and found out that my entire family perished in the camps. Not a single person left."

She dabbed at her eyes and Stan couldn't help but grab her other hand and say, "I'm so sorry."

"It is what it is." Agnieska's cracking voice belied her brave face. "I couldn't find any records about Janusz. But they told me both you and Peter had been prisoners of war.

211

So I came here in the hopes of finding someone." She leaned back in the chair and a tiny smile appeared on her lips. "I'm so glad I found you."

"Me, too." Stan's heart felt lighter than it had in years. He admired her strength in the face of impossible odds, and he loved the way she'd managed to stay positive despite all the evil she'd experienced. "You can stay here for as long as you wish."

"I couldn't possibly impose on you."

"You're not imposing," he said, afraid she'd leave him alone again. "You hid my nephew Janusz for almost two years and saved his life. Everyone in my family is indebted to you forever."

"He's my nephew, too," she reminded him and a sweet laughter fell from her lips. "But thanks for the offer. I'll stay – but only until I have found a place for myself."

Stan hoped she'd never find another place to stay. "Come, I'll show you around."

"I love what you've done with the place," she said with a laugh, looking at the utter destruction.

"Really? It's post-war fashion," Stan chuckled, the tension of the past months slowly dissipating. "For now I've been sleeping in the shed but I'll ask someone to repair the roof so you can have a proper house."

Agnieska gave him a scrutinizing glance and asked, "Why don't you do it yourself? I remember you and Jarek were always clambering up on the roof."

The mention of his twin brother sent a pang of jealousy into his heart. Back then, before the war, Agnieska had had a serious crush on his brother. Not on him.

When he didn't answer, she looked pointedly at his leg and asked, "What happened?"

He pondered lying for a moment, but then opted for the truth. "Amputated."

"I almost didn't notice the limp," she said as if it were the most normal thing in the world that a man had only one leg. Maybe it was. More and more maimed soldiers came home from the battlefields and the prison camps with one or more missing limbs.

"For now you can sleep here." He pointed at the only intact place in the house, beneath the stairs. It was just big enough to place a mattress there.

"I've had worse," she said and dropped her satchel on the ground. "It's not that I have a lot of luggage either." Again she smiled, sending hot chills up and down his spine.

Stan looked away. "The stove is working and there's still some canned food in the pantry beneath the kitchen. I've been doing my best growing vegetables and sowing crops for the coming winter, but I can do only so much."

"Now you have me to help," Agnieska said, her enthusiastic voice drawing him to her like a moth to the flame. He told himself it was only because two persons could achieve more than one.

"I'm still hoping Katrina and Richard will find their way home," he said to distract himself from gazing at Agnieska's enticing lips.

"And they will as soon as they can. Just like I did. You'll see they are fine," she said, putting a hand on his arm.

Agnieska rolled up her sleeves and under her capable hands, with the help of hired workers from the village, the farmhouse returned to its former beauty. Stan worked on the field with Tadzio, while she tended to the vegetable and herb garden, growing enough food for themselves and to pay for the hired work.

But Stan knew that they still needed to grow more if they wanted to eat during the winter.

~

Several weeks passed and the two of them had moved upstairs, Stan into the room he'd occupied with his brothers and Agnieska into the other room that had been Katrina's as a child. One day he found her in the kitchen, sitting on the floor with a faded photograph in her hands, tears streaming down her cheeks.

"Agnieska, what's wrong?" He took the photograph from her hands. It showed Peter and her sister Ludmila at their wedding. She must have found it somewhere amongst the rubble, because it was dusty with burned edges.

More tears streamed down, as she cleared her throat several times, trying to talk. Stan let himself slide down beside her with some difficulty and wrapped an arm around her. Much to his surprise, she leaned into his chest.

"I'm the only one who survived," she sobbed against his chest, only to expel herself from his embrace and glare daggers at him, before she pummeled her fists into him, sobbing, "Why? Why me? Why not them?"

"Because Richard rescued you," Stan reminded her.

"He shouldn't have. I don't deserve it. He should have rescued someone else, someone more important, worthier of survival. I'm just a simple housewife," Agnieska cried.

"You're not. You're the strongest, most determined person I've ever come across. You saved Janusz. And me..."

"You?" Her eyes rounded with surprise. "You didn't need me. You've been doing well on your own."

"Maybe. But I was lonely. Depressed. You brought the sunshine back into my life," he whispered, half-ashamed of the cheesy words. But it was the truth. Without Agnieska, he didn't know whether he'd have wanted to toil on.

Agnieska got to her feet and then helped Stan up as well. "I'm sorry for my outburst."

"It happens to all of us." He remembered the day when he arrived at the farm and drank himself into unconsciousness, weeping all night. "Why don't you rest for a few hours..."

"No, I'd rather stay busy. Keep my mind busy."

A few days later, while eating dinner, Stan and Agnieska talked about the future.

Stan said, "We should have enough food come winter and with any luck we can hunt deer in the fall. That'll get us some meat."

Agnieska cast her eyes downward. Since her breakdown, there had been an awkward tension between them. "I'm not sure whether I should stay..."

"Are you planning to leave?" Stan asked, an icy hand grabbing his heart. He'd grown so used to having her around, seeing her smile, hearing her cheerful voice. He couldn't possibly fathom a life without her.

"Would you even have me any longer? I feel like I've imposed for too long..." she said with a soft voice.

"It's been nice having you here. Please stay," Stan answered.

Agnieska gave him a curious look but said nothing else and the rest of the week she avoided his presence as best as she could. He started to believe that he'd somehow misread her signals and overstepped with his insinuation of liking her around.

A week later, she sought him out while he worked in the field. "What can I help you with?"

"Don't you have something else you'd rather be doing than helping me outside?" Stan asked with surprise.

"No. I need to be outside for a while."

He handed her a shovel and showed her how he to create the rows for the vegetables to grow. Agnieska watched for a minute and then mimicked his actions. "Like this?"

"Yes. That's right."

They worked silently side by side for a few minutes before she said, "I used to be afraid of you."

"What?" Stan asked, and leaned on his shovel, scrutinizing her face.

"When we were younger, I was afraid of you." Her voice was but a whisper and she didn't dare look into his eyes.

"Why?"

"Because of your temper. Every girl in Lodz was afraid of you, except for your sister," she glanced at him, but quickly looked away.

Stan felt a pang of guilt. He hadn't known that Agnieska had been afraid of him. He'd been famous for his rash temper, yes, but he'd never thought a girl would shrink away from him because of it.

"Are you still afraid of me?" he asked.

A cute flush stained her cheeks pink. "Not any more."

"Do you still have a crush on Jarek?"

The pink turned into beet-red. "Jarek is dead. That would be pointless, don't you think?"

"I don't know. You always followed him around like a puppy." Stan shrugged.

"That was a long time ago. We're not adolescents any longer. I'm twenty-four now."

"And I'm twenty-six. Did you forget we are almost the same age?" Stan asked, looking her up and down and wondering what she would do if he kissed her.

Agnieska dropped her shovel and clasped her hands together in front of her, "I haven't forgotten anything. At first, I admit I saw Jarek whenever I looked at you, but that barely lasted a few days. You and the Jarek I knew are nothing alike. You have matured so much. You've grown and become a kind and generous man. Determined to eke out a better future for yourself and your family against all odds, braving the hardships. I admire your strength."

Stan nodded and took an experimental step towards her. When she didn't move back, he took another, until they were only a few inches apart. "You're beautiful."

"I am?" she asked, lifting her head and meeting his eyes for the first time since coming to join him outside.

He lifted a hand and let her hair waterfall through his fingers. It felt like strands of silk and glimmered as the sun shone down on it. "I want to kiss you."

Agnieska widened her eyes and shyly nodded her assent. Stan cupped her jaw, letting his hand slip behind her neck. With his other hand he tipped her chin upwards and gently touched his lips to her own. She kept her hands at her sides, but despite the distance between them, Stan could feel her tremble.

He kissed her again, this time more passionately and relished with joy the moment she surrendered and leaned into his body. He wrapped her in his arms, continuing to kiss her, but he couldn't dispel her nervousness.

"Do you want me to stop?" he asked. When she shook her head, he took her hands and placed them on his shoulders. "Hold me."

Agnieska bit her bottom lip, but ever so slowly, her hands crept over his shoulders and touched the nape of his neck. When she pushed her fingers into his hair, Stan groaned and closed his eyes to savor the sensation her hands were creating. It had been such a long time since he'd been with a woman. Between hiding from the enemy, working for the resistance, and being held a prisoner, relationships had been low on his priority list.

He'd been falling in love with her for the last few weeks, but he'd been afraid to act on his feelings for fear she would only see his dead twin instead of him. Now that he knew, he couldn't wait to make her his.

"Won't you regret being with a …" He couldn't bring himself to say the word. "…a man with only one leg?"

She smiled at him. When he nodded, she reached up and clasped his face between her hands. "I'm sorry for the pain and suffering you went through, but you're more man with only one leg than thousands of others with both legs. You're made of the kind of material real heroes are made of."

Stan was touched by her comments and kissed her again.

"Will you marry me, Agnieska?" he asked on an impulse, breaking their kiss.

She stared at him in surprise and then started laughing. "Right now?"

"If you wish."

"Yes, I will. Let's go into town and get married." She continued to laugh. "I never expected you to propose to me. Even less after our first kiss, but I'll take you any time of the day. I love you, Stanislaw Zdanek."

"I love you too, future Mrs. Zdanek."

The War Girl series continues with Richard and Katrina, as they have to flee from the Red Army after the murder of Bartosz's mother. They hide with friends, but as the war draws to an end and the hunting season for Germans opens, it takes only one betrayal to toss Richard – and Katrina by affiliation – into the worst of persecution.

Buy **Bitter Tears** right now!

And since I fell in love with Stan and Agnieska so much, I wrote an entire book about them falling in love with each other. Mind you, this is a romance novel that focuses on their relationship, exploring the struggles each of them has to overcome to find together.

It's written in alternating point of views of Stan and Agnieska. If you're dying to know how she thinks about this grumpy, bitter, yet endearing man, then Second Chance at First Love is for you.

Buy here: Second Chance at First Love

AUTHOR'S NOTES

Dear Reader,

Thanks so much for reading UNCOMMON SACRIFICE, I hope you enjoyed the book.

After sending Peter off to a POW camp at the end of Fatal Encounter, I initially had a "nice", albeit uncomfortable stay in a prison camp in mind for him. But during my research I came across very disturbing information on the website of the Bergen-Belsen concentration camp memorial about the infamous death marches.

About five hundred male Home Army officers suffered a horrible odyssey: they were shipped to the camp Gross Born in Pomerania by train and after only nine days stay, they were put on a grueling march back to the West. The survivors reached Sandbostel about two months later – less than seventy miles away from Fallingbostel where they'd started their dreadful journey. But the poor souls hadn't suffered enough yet and were once again set in motion until they reached Lübeck, where they were finally liberated by the British Arm.

While Uncommon Sacrifice is obviously a work of fiction, Peter's ordeal retraced the steps of real-life prisoners being forced on the same march.

I want to give a huge thanks to Kevin Greenhalgh, curator of the Fallingbostel Military Museum, who gave me a personal tour through the museum and graciously gifted me with two editions of the National Ex-Prisoner of War Association's magazine. These excellent publications are filled with invaluable information, including eyewitness reports from the death marches and prison life. If you ever happen to be near Hannover, Germany you should take the opportunity to visit the museum.

If you have read Trouble Brewing, you will remember Stan, the gruff, snarky and short-tempered partisan who hates everything German with a passion. I couldn't resist throwing him into German captivity, corroborating his prejudices and fueling his hatred. But I think he redeems himself rather nicely in the end.

Throughout the book I grew to love Stan, and wanted to give him a happy ending. Agnieska was just the perfect woman for him. Since I'm a romantic at heart, I decided to dedicate an entire romance novel to the story of how Stan and Agnieska fall in love with each other. It's called Second Chance at First Love.

I struggled a long time over whether to include the scene where Anna and her mother are raped by the Russian soldiers. In the end I decided to include it, because it wouldn't be historically accurate to miraculously let her get away unscathed.

An estimated 3-4 million German women were raped after the war by the Allied forces. Most notorious were the Russians, but the other nations did their share of awful things, too. In Berlin during May and June 1945 rape became such a routine that the women eventually ignored it and even laughed it off, as long as it wasn't accompanied by additional violence. This grim sense of humor is expressed in the saying *Better an Ivan (Russian) on the belly than a Yank on the head*, which means that being raped is preferable to being blown up by a bomb. Obviously not all women were able to shrug off the horrific crimes against them and thousands upon thousands committed suicide to escape the situation.

If you are wondering whether Professor Scherer's strategy of dispensing favors would have worked in real life, the answer is: unfortunately, yes. There are many reports of Nazis, even the worst kind, who stayed unpunished. The Allies closed both eyes to the crimes committed by those that were useful to them, or those that had been wise enough to collect goodwill with the later victors.

Of course I couldn't have written this book without the help of so many special people. As always, I want to thank my fantastic cover designer Daniela Colleo from stunningbookcovers.com, my editor Tami Stark, and my proofreaders Martin O' Hearn and JJ Toner.

Special thanks go to Michael J. McKenzie, a combat veteran and now author of a semi-autobiographic series of the war in Iraq called On the Way. He graciously helped me to make the battle scenes in the first chapters as realistic as possible.

ALSO BY MARION KUMMEROW

Love and Resistance in WW2 Germany

Unrelenting

Unyielding

Unwavering

War Girl Series

Downed over Germany (Prequel)

War Girl Ursula (Book 1)

War Girl Lotte (Book 2)

War Girl Anna (Book 3)

Trouble Brewing (Book 4)

Fatal Encounter (Book 5)

Uncommon Sacrifice (Book 6)

Bitter Tears (Book 7)

Secrets Revealed (Book 8)

Together at Last (Book 9)

Endless Ordeal (Book 10)

Historical Romance

Second Chance at First Love

Find all my books here:

http://www.kummerow.info

CONTACT ME

I truly appreciate you taking the time to read (and enjoy) my books. And I'd be thrilled to hear from you!
If you'd like to get in touch with me you can do so via

Twitter:
http://twitter.com/MarionKummerow

Facebook:
http://www.facebook.com/AutorinKummerow

Website
http://www.kummerow.info

Printed in Great Britain
by Amazon